NEECEY'S LULLABY

a novel

CRIS BURKS

HARLEM MOON

broadway books

new york

Published by Harlem Moon, an imprint of Broadway Books, a division of Random House, Inc.

PRINTED IN THE UNITED STATES OF AMERICA

HARLEM MOON, BROADWAY BOOKS, and the HARLEM MOON logo, depicting a moon and a woman, are trademarks of Random House, Inc. The figure in the Harlem Moon logo is inspired by a graphic design by Aaron Douglas (1899–1979).

Visit our Web site at www.harlemmoon.com

First edition published 2005

Book design by Elizabeth Rendfleisch

The cataloging-in-publication data is on file at the library of Congress.

ISBN 0-7679-1983-1

10 9 8 7 6 5 4 3 2 1

To my sons, Tyrone, Brian, Royce, and Roman:

The past does not control us

The past does not control us

The past does not control us . . .

ACKNOWLEDGMENTS AND THANKS

Some chapters in this novel have appeared in *Emergence: A Journal of Women Writing, Short Fiction by Women, Hair Trigger 14, The Thing About Love,* and *The Thing About Second Chances.* The poem *Scars* was first published by *Shooting Star Review.*

Special thanks to Gary Johnson, my graduate adviser at Columbia College, Chicago, for his support and insight in shaping this novel. I'm always grateful to Michelle Amor for her artistic support, Kay Hankins for her unending encouragement, Brandy Johnson for being my rear guard, and Marjorie Taylor for being a sister in a time of trouble. I had a wonderful editing experience with Clarence Haynes at Harlem Moon. Clarence, your questions forced me to dig a little deeper. Many thanks to Victoria Sanders, my agent, for her continuous support.

Finally, but most important, to my husband, Royce: Thank you for putting up with my insomnia and wackiness. In you, I found a perfect resting place.

SCARS

One hundred and seven scars
    zagging across my body
Here on my right kneecap
    the hot licks of an extension cord
Here on the left shoulder
    the steel imprint of a kitchen chair
Sorrow sings along the baseboards
    walls crash around me
Dark passages in my mother's house
    a child's dream found in fairy tales
Purge me of my sins, mother
    make me obedient
Here's my faith
    autograph it with keloids
There are one hundred and seven scars
    none accidental

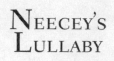

NEECEY'S LULLABY

chapter 1

THE FAMILY SONG

*i*N JUNE OF 1956, the South Towne Movie Theater sat on Sixty-third and Emerald like an old terra-cotta southwestern fort—the Alamo or Fort Worth. On Saturday afternoons, kids flocked to the theater while adults flocked to Sears Roebuck, F. W. Woolworth's, Wiebolt's, and other stores on Halsted Street. The blare of traffic and the chatter of voices fused with the clickety-clack of the Englewood-Howard el. Whites and blacks mingled and went about their weekly shopping and business transactions as if they had co-inhabited Englewood for generations.

In 1956, seven-year-old Neecey's universe converged on Sixty-third and Halsted. After the Chicago winter curled itself into sleep, she and her daddy, Jesse, walked the five blocks from Sixtieth and Peoria to the bustling business district. They stopped at Fannie May's and purchased a box of fruit fudge for her mama, Ruby. They stopped at F. W. Woolworth's for a hot dog, french fries, and cola. The latest edition of *Superman* comics was added to a pile of purchases: aspirin, a bag of steel wool, a bottle of Griffin White Shoe Polish, and finally the doughnuts.

The sweet greasy aroma slithered from the shop underneath the el tracks, looped around Jesse and Neecey, and tugged them into the long narrow room. The doughnut shop, always packed to capacity, pulsated with voices that competed with the rumbling el. Rows and rows of glazed, powdered, and coconut doughnuts, chocolate éclairs, and Bavarian creams sat in the glass cases that separated the blue-haired white women from the onslaught of customers. The women rushed up and down their tiny aisle from the large silver coffee urns, to the milk case, to the doughnut racks, and to the cash register. They grabbed money from the drooling men, women, and children while passing bags of greasy doughnuts to them. Once Jesse and Neecey purchased the doughnuts they left the shop and headed for home.

"Watch that hole, Daddy, the ground'll swallow you!" Neecey warned as she jumped across a grate in the sidewalk. Her cork brown knees and legs glistened with Vaseline petroleum jelly. Two of her three thick braids bounced against her shoulders. Her front braid brushed against her face and wiped the glaze from the corner of her mouth.

Jesse laughed as she leaped across grates and manholes. He was a short, muscular man with tiny feet. His caramel eyes sparkled beneath eyebrows as thick and black as electrical tape. His round nose sloped over a pencil-thin mustache and small lips. His mouth turned down in a crooked smile. His brown skin reminded Neecey of golden brown corn bread. When Neecey held his hand, she felt his callused fingertips against her skin. But always, when he touched her face, his hands were gentle.

The stores disappeared behind them as they made their way home, jumping across manholes, skipping over cracks in the sidewalks, laughing, running, waving at bus drivers, and oohing over fancy cars—Buicks, Chevrolets, or Cadillacs that soared down the street like big birds. When they turned off busy Halsted Street into their quiet neighborhood, women working in their gardens exclaimed, "What a pretty little girl!"

Neecey giggled and clasped Jesse's hands. Yes, she was her daddy's pretty girl—a thin girl with a long oval face. Her hazel eyes questioned everything. Her nose commanded the center of her face, while her lips, thick and full, spread in a continuous smile. Jesse called her his li'l cutie pie. Because she was happy to be so *cute* and her daddy's little girl, Neecey skipped ahead of him, singing *Skip, skip, skip to my Lou.*

Her small squeaky voice rose and disturbed the quietness of that Saturday morning. Jesse, knowing the child could not carry a tune and would never be able to sing a decent note, lifted his bushy eyebrows and grimaced at the women. When they approached their gray stone building, Neecey spied her Uncle Pete leaning against the wide gray column and puffing on his pipe. She ran the last few yards, yelling "Uncle Pete! Uncle Pete!"

"How was yo' trip, honey bun?" He laughed. His narrow eyes sparkled under a thicket of eyebrows. Pete and Jesse's eyes and lips announced to the world that they were brothers, but the resemblance ended with the thick eyebrows, caramel eyes, and small lips. Pete had a pointy head like a football and a parrot nose that hooked over his tiny lips. Jesse's was compact and round. Pete was tall and angular. Jesse had small feet. Pete had large feet that always appeared to be moving in different directions.

"What kinda doughnuts you get today?" Pete asked.

"Glazed! Glazed, Uncle Pete!" She laughed and widened her big round eyes.

"Glazed." Pete laughed and scooped her up. He spun her around. Her legs flew out like kite tails.

"Aaah, ha, ha, ha, ha!" She laughed. "Put me down, Uncle Pete. Ha, ha, ha. Put me down."

"Don't make her throw up," Jesse warned as he walked up the steps.

"Glaze doughnuts coming in for a landing," Pete said as he lowered her to the porch. He stooped and pulled a big white handkerchief from his back pocket. "You better wipe that glaze from yo' mouth before yo' Auntie Della sees it and has a hissie-fit."

"Laud, Jesse," Pete imitated Della's voice. "You ain't got good sense, giving this child sweets before lunch."

Neecey laughed and grabbed his cheeks. She watched his mustache stretch into a thin black line across his face. "Auntie Della," she said. "Whada big mustache you got."

"Honey bun, yo' hands are sticky, too!" Pete said in his own voice.

Jesse laughed. "I thought we could sneak past Della today."

"She's sitting at the dining room table with her Bible opened," Pete warned as he rubbed his handkerchief across Neecey's hands. "You ain't getting past her today. And man, you gonna catch the Sox game with me or what?"

"Be ready before you can say Jackie Robinson." Jesse laughed. "Let me get the kids taken care of."

Neecey and Jesse stepped into a jungle of houseplants—philodendrons, rubber tree plants, and mother-in-law tongues. The jungle separated the dining room from the living room with its furniture sheathed in plastic. A door off the living room led into Pete and Della's bedroom. Pete's wife, Della, sat at the dining room table with her eyeglasses perched on the tip of her nose and an open Bible on the table. Behind her was a door leading into the bedroom that Jesse shared with his wife and three children. The center of the plants rustled. Neecey spied the bright red shirt of her four-year-old brother, Jack.

"Ssssshhh!" Jesse said.

"Aaargh," a tiny voice came from the plants.

"Daddy, Daddy." Neecey clutched Jesse's leg. "Itsa monster!"

"Aaaaarrrrgh," Jack said. He walked out of the plants with his arms held high above his head and his hands bent like claws. He resembled Jesse, from his thick, wavy hair to the small frame of his body.

"Get 'im, Daddy!" Neecey cried and hid behind Jesse.

"Take the bag, sweetie," he said and shoved the package at Neecey.

She wrapped her skinny arms around the large bag and placed her chin upon the box of doughnuts. Jesse dashed forward and scooped up Jack.

"I got the monster!" he shouted.

"I swear, Jesse," Della said as she looked up from the Bible. Her bat eyes peered over her glasses. "You're worse than a child."

"You're worse than an old snot, Della." He laughed.

Like Pete, Della was all bones and angles. While Pete was a soft playful brown, Della was a dark, hard brown. Her shirtwaist dresses lay against her chest like linen on a table. Her small breasts were puckers that didn't hold much promise of pleasure. Her arms and legs were as skinny as new saplings. Neecey noticed that, as usual, Della was rubbing her left toes around the ankle of her right foot. Her pencil-thin eyebrows narrowed into a *V*. Her small eyes seemed to disappear in their sockets.

"How many doughnuts you let this child eat?" she asked Jesse.

"About six," he lied and set Jack on the floor.

He took the packages from Neecey and started past Della,

but twenty-two-month-old Odessa wandered out of the bedroom with a bottle dangling from her mouth. She saw Jesse, and her eyes widened. She popped the bottle from her mouth and ran to him.

Jesse swept her up with his free arm and imitated W. C. Fields. "My Li'l Chickadee." He walked past Della with Jack on his heels.

"Come here, Neecey," Della beckoned as Neecey passed her. She turned the Sunday school book over onto the Bible and drew Neecey to her. She lifted the thick braid that hung down the side of Neecey's face. Her fingers were rough and hard like Jesse's.

"Got glaze all in this child's hair!" Della called to Jesse.

Della rubbed the braid between her forefinger and thumb as she stared into the child's almond-shaped eyes. "Honey, you gotta learn to say no thank you or you gonna be Auntie's fat dumpling."

Neecey looked into Della's little eyes, "I only ate two, Auntie."

"Two is too much sugar for a li'l girl. I 'spect you won't eat a bite of lunch." Della pushed her glasses up on her face.

"Ain't hungry," Neecey said.

"Jesse!" Della shouted down the hall. "You hear this? She ain't hungry. You filled her with all that sugar and ruined her lunch."

"Della, she had a hot dog." Jesse returned from the kitchen.

"Hmph, and a Coca-Cola and french fries and probably a couple of Pay Days!" Della shouted and rose from the table.

"Only ate one Pay Day, Auntie." Neecey stepped back and looked up at the tall tree of a woman.

"That's too much sugar!" Della exclaimed. "You're gonna drink a glass of milk right now."

Milk was Della's cure-all. Della grabbed Neccey's hand and pulled her down the hall. As they passed the bedroom, Neecey saw her mother lying with her back to the door. Her arm rested upon her large beach ball belly.

Perspiration ran down Ruby's face. She felt the sweat attacking each of her red pin curls. Nevertheless, she refused to get up and open the window, refused to let *them* know she was awake. *Children everywhere*, she thought and rubbed her belly. She hummed a few bars of "God Bless the Child," then stopped. She closed her eyes and listened to the family scurrying around the kitchen table.

The kitchen was a wide room with a large pine table in the center. Although the dining room could have easily held all the members of the family, it was in this kitchen that everyone gathered for meals, news of the day, a game of Spades, or Candyland with the children. Neecey scrambled into the chair next to Jack. Jesse, with a dish towel slung across his shoulder, strained to open a jar of sandwich spread. A loaf of bread and a pack of bologna lay on the table next to a small tray with a sugar bowl, creamer, and condiments.

"Why don't you go on to the game?" Della said. "I can fix these kids some lunch."

"You're sure, Della?" He looked at her as he twisted off the top.

"Go on," she said. She leaned across the table and took the jar from him.

"Thanks," he said and shoved the sandwich fixings across the table.

A bedroom door swung open, and Louise stormed out. She

was a tall dark woman with long dark hair that hung in waves around her shoulders. She threw her hands out as if directing a choir. The hanging flab of her upper arms flapped like flags in a breeze.

"Thanks?" she barked. "Thanks? You need to get that lazy wife of yours up!"

"Ma'Dear, don't start on Ruby," Jesse said as he removed the towel from his shoulder. "She gotta take it easy. Losing this baby would be hard on her."

"Hard?" Louise sneered as she stormed across the room to the sink. "She don't want none of . . ."

"Louise!" Della interjected. She looked pointedly at the children. "Why you wanna talk about folks in front of kids, I'll never know."

"Soon she won't be able to," Jesse said and flung the towel over Louise's head to the sink.

"Don't think I'm gonna sweat tears because y'all move out," Louise said and pulled a coffee cup from the cabinet over the sink. She turned to the stove and poured lukewarm coffee into her cup.

"Go on, Jesse," Della said as she slapped the sandwich spread on a slice of bread. "I'll take care of the kids 'til you get back."

"Thanks again, Della," Jesse said. "And you, Ma'Dear, don't start no bull in front of my children."

"You coulda done so much . . ."

"I said no bull, Ma'Dear," he warned. "Promise me."

"Yeah, yeah," Louise said and took three gulps of coffee.

"Be good," Jesse said to the children.

"Okay, Daddy," Neecey said and set her long face on her hands.

Louise grimaced as he kissed the top of Neecey's head.

She downed the rest of her coffee as he ruffled Jack's head and then kissed Odessa. He looked in her face as he moved around the table. He stood in front of her and smiled his crooked smile.

"Be a good girl, Louise," he said and chucked her double chin.

She lifted her head and tried to fake a frown. He dropped a kiss on her forehead.

"Go on," she said. "Go on before you miss the first ball."

"Thanks again, Della," he said and left the room.

Della set saucers with sandwiches before Jack and Odessa while keeping an eye on Louise. Louise pulled a face cloth from the pocket of her housedress, turned to the sink, and wet her towel under the running water.

"Why can't you just go to the bathroom and wash yo' face like everybody else?" Della asked as she twisted the top on the jar of sandwich spread.

"Why I gotta be a second-class citizen in my own home?" Louise asked. "I should be able to do any damn thing I want to."

Della's small bat eyes widened. "Louise!"

"Oh, Della," Louise said and wiped the towel across her face and in the corner of her eyes. "You don't shock that easily . . ."

"Naw, but you got grandchildren at the table," Della said. "And I don't want you talking like that around them."

Louise looked at her and nodded. Della's eyes had narrowed to slits. Louise did not want to upset this daughter-in-law who itched to give her a *God-don't-like-ugly* sermon. If it had been anyone else but Della, Louise would have told them to get the hell out of her face. But Della was not Ruby, who slept all day and made Jesse wait on her hand and foot. Della was Louise's Ruth and, like that biblical Ruth, she was a good wife to Pete and a good daughter in-law to Louise. She had no secret past, no outside children.

"Yeah," Louise said and looked pointedly at Della, "I do have *some* grandchildren at the table."

"Louise, you promised Jesse."

"Yeah," Louise said. "Don't wanna upset the queen bee."

THAT NIGHT, Neecey and her family squeezed into their packed bedroom. Jack snored from behind Neecey on the small cot that they shared. Ruby sat on the edge of the full-size bed she shared with Jesse and Odessa. Her blue peignoir over her pregnant stomach resembled a pile of whipped topping. The lamp on the nightstand cast a soft yellow glow across the bed, and Jesse leaned into the light with the latest issue of *Jet* magazine. Odessa lay in the crook created by his curved body. It was a typical evening, with Neecey watching her mother kit-curl her hair. Ruby's fingers sectioned hair and twisted that section into a circle. She crisscrossed two bobby pins into each curl. There were moments Neecey wanted to climb into Ruby's lap and touch her small nose. She wanted to say *You're so pretty, Mama.* Her mother's skin was like coffee with too much cream. Her gray eyes were slanted like the eyes of the small Chinese doll locked in the dining room hutch.

"I don't wanna move none of this crap," Ruby said as she twisted the last curl. From her cot, Neecey watched Ruby's mouth move as fast as her flying fingers. "And don't think all yo' hoodlum buddies gonna be running in and out of my place. We gonna have something decent for these kids."

"Don't start building no jail to keep me in," Jesse warned and slammed the magazine on the nightstand.

"You wanna be free," Ruby snapped.

Jesse didn't answer. Ruby rose and jerked the top sheet back on the bed. She slipped beneath the sheet, turned her back to Jesse, and hugged her pillow.

"Goodnight, sweetie," Jesse called to Neecey.

"'Night, Daddy," Neecey answered and snuggled into her pillow.

Jesse clicked off the lamp. Darkness and silence descended like a heavy hand. Neecey listened to the silence and drifted off to sleep long before Jesse's hands found Ruby's soft breasts and long before Ruby's forgiveness came in the parting of her thighs.

That Saturday always played in Neecey's mind. It was a reminder of the time in her life when her happiness was as sweet as glazed doughnuts.

chapter 2

THE DADDY DIRGE

*I*N AUGUST OF 1956, Jesse and Pete, punch press operators at Pacer Factory, began working overtime on Saturdays. Neecey spent those Saturdays with her friend Trisha. Sometimes they pretended to cook turnip greens (grass with rocks placed upon Trisha's tea set), sugar cookies (mud pies), and Kool-Aid drinks (water mixed with a little dirt). They jumped rope . . . *Mabel, Mabel, set the table, don't forget your red-hot peas . . .*

Or ripped and ran up and down Peoria and the alley until dusk, when the parents came out on their stoops and sang out to the children: "Tris-sss-sha!" "Neee-ceeey!" "Freeed!" "Peaaanut!"

And the children scattered to their homes for dinner. Later, as the evening sun cast an orange blush onto the gray stone buildings, as the trees rustled gently, and the tinkling bell of the ice-cream pushcart drifted down the serene street, the families eased out of their apartments onto the stoops. The children chased fireflies, and the parents gossiped. The red tips of cigarettes glowed, and the air was sweet with the scent of freshly cut grass.

This particular Saturday, Trisha's sister, seventeen-year-old Freda, and her friends Thelma and Paula took the girls to the matinee at the South Towne. They sat through cartoons and the double feature while popcorn and candy flew across the theater. Teenagers necked in the balcony while children ran up and down the aisles until an usher escorted them out. At 5:30, the theater doors opened. A mob of children poured out of the show and dispersed in four directions. Neecey's group walked over to Halsted and up to Sixty-first Street.

"Always something to see on Halsted," Freda said and pointed to a platinum blonde white woman with eyes laden with blue eye shadow and black eyelashes as thick as whisk brooms.

"Laud ha'mercy!" Thelma cried and pointed to a woman with an elephant-wide rump stuffed in a skin-tight red skirt that crept down her trunk legs. The girls laughed as the woman took baby steps in her sky-high heels.

"Naw, girl," Paula said, "look at that fool." She pointed to an old man with greasy white hair wearing a tobacco-stained T-shirt and a black leather jacket. "It's ninety degrees in the shade, and that fool's dressed for ice."

And so it went. No one mentioned Thelma's pointy, large breasts, which spilled over the cups of her bra and made lumps and ridges in her skin-tight sweater. No one spoke of Freda's large shapeless legs, which sat in her shoes like elephant trunks. No one dared snicker at Paula's narrow feet in her Olive Oyl shoes.

If the girls' attention had not been diverted by an airplane overhead, skywriting in fluffy letters, Y-A-H-O-O, they would have immediately noticed the man at the bus stop on Sixty-first and Halsted. His yellowed gray hair poked from underneath a wide-brimmed straw hat. From his matted beard to his wrinkled seersucker suit, the man looked as if he had just rolled out of bed. He clasped a photograph in one hand and an envelope, which he studied, in the other. When he spied the girls walking toward him, a visible jolt went through his body. He looked at the photograph, then at Neecey. He slipped the picture and envelope into his jacket pocket and waited for the girls. The girls, fascinated by the letters, walked with their heads tilted. Not one of them noticed the man's keen interest in their group. They were startled when he spoke to Neecey.

"Pamela Denise?" He smiled.

Only her mother called her Pamela Denise, and always, that name was followed by a command: *Pamela Denise, sit yo' butt down. Pamela Denise, don't you dare touch those cookies. Pamela Denise, go to bed.* No one else called her that.

"You know him, Neecey?" Freda asked as she draped a protective arm around Neecey's shoulder.

Neecey shook her head. She did not know this man, who resembled a yellow bogeyman. His hazel eyes bulged from his head, and his hands hung from his sleeves like shovels.

"I'm yo' daddy," the man said and walked toward her.

"Mister," Freda said as she pushed Neecey behind her, "we know her daddy, and you ain't him."

The man walked toward Freda. Paula and Thelma closed ranks in front of Freda. Trisha put her arm around Neecey.

"Mister, if you don't leave this girl alone, we gonna start screaming," Paula warned. "Let's go, y'all."

She walked between the group and the man. She stood for a moment and looked defiantly in his face. Her wide plump face was close to his. The other girls eased around them. Thelma, who was a short dumpy girl, pulled Trisha close to her and rushed past the man. The man, frozen by the threat of screaming girls, watched them go.

"You some kinda creep?" Paula yelled as she hurried away. "Messing with little girls?"

"You don't know him, Neecey?" Freda asked.

Neecey shook her head. Her daddy was Jesse. *Pretty Jesse,* Ruby often teased, *got all the women sniffing around my door like hounds.* She glanced back at the man. A shiver of fear ran down her spine. The man was taking slow, easy steps behind them.

Neecey grabbed Freda's hand. *Don't let that bogeyman get me,* she thought and squeezed Freda's hand.

"Walk faster, y'all," Paula said. "He's following us."

"When I tell y'all to run, run," Freda whispered. She pushed Neecey ahead of her.

They rushed across Sixty-first Street. An occasional car zoomed past the girls. The smell of charcoal drifted from a yard. A dog barked. A baby cried from a building. Freda glanced over her shoulder as they crossed Greene Street. Now the man was much closer.

"Run!" Freda hissed, and the girls broke into a run.

Neecey heard drums in her ears. Her knees were weak, and her legs were wobbly. Fear oozed from the top of her head to the soles of her feet, yet she kept running. Tears streamed down her face. She wanted to look back, but if she did the bogeyman would reach out and snatch her. She would never see her real daddy again. Twice Freda tugged her arm.

"Paula, Thelma, y'all get Trisha to my house," Freda shouted.

Paula and Thelma grabbed the smaller girl's hands. They skirted around a tricycle in the middle of the sidewalk. Freda stumbled over the tricycle and lost her hold on Neecey's hand. Freda's hands shot out to protect her face. The handlebars of the tricycle caught her in the stomach. A pedal knocked against her leg. She landed on the concrete. Pain swept from her elbows and arms through her legs. Neecey sidestepped the tricycle and paused, unsure of what to do, but Freda yelled, "Run, Neecey, run!"

"Mama, Mama!" Neecey screamed as she skirted around Freda and the tricycle. "Mama, Mama!"

Neecey bounded up the narrow concrete steps to the wide porch and fell upon the doorbell. A thousand times she pushed the bell. A thousand hours passed and finally the door opened. Ruby stepped onto the porch. Her fingers and blue-and-white maternity top were covered with flour. Sweat ran from her sherry red hair down the slope of her nose.

"What's the matter with you?" she asked, dusting the flour from her hands.

Neecey wrapped her arms around Ruby's waist.

"Neecey, get off me!" Ruby pushed the child's arms away.

"That man!" Neecey cried and pointed to the man a few yards away from the building. "That man says he's my daddy."

For Ruby, the moment slowed to a hard frame. Milton Beasley, her first husband, stood at the bottom of the stairs. Shock, recognition, anger, relief, wave after wave of emotions washed across his face while only terror gripped Ruby. She heard the expression *My Laud* come from somewhere inside herself. The man's eyes never left her face as his legs rose slowly from the ground and his foot touched the first steps. She felt her hands—they must be her hands—clawing at Neecey's arms. His thin lips stretched across his stained teeth. His wide hands reached toward her, toward Neecey.

"Ruby," he whispered, and shattered time.

Now, Ruby could move. She grabbed Neecey and flung her toward the door. Neecey collided with the doorjamb. A hard pain racked her shoulder blade. The man grabbed Ruby, pulled her to him, and wrapped his arms around her. She struggled to get out of his embrace. She squirmed in his arms. His hat fell from his head.

"Ruby," he whispered.

"Mama! Mama!" Neecey cried.

"Get inside the house and lock the door!" Ruby shouted.

Neecey stumbled into the vestibule, flew into the apartment, closed and locked the door. She raced through the apartment shouting, "Auntie, Ma'Dear!"

The aroma of frying chicken filled the apartment, but the quiet was deep. No one else was home. Neecey rushed back to the living room. She pushed aside the lace curtains. On the front stoop, Ruby still struggled against the man. She stomped his foot, and he released her. Ruby backed away from the man. She wiped her hands nervously down the sides of her blue maternity skirt and left white streaks of flour.

"You got no business here, Mr. Milton."

"That's my daughter," Mr. Milton said. He bent and picked up his hat. He held it like an offering plate. His face and arms were covered with flour from his struggle with Ruby. People in the neighboring two-flat buildings poured onto their porches. On the sidewalk below them, Freda hobbled up the walk. Blood streamed from her thick right leg. Her mother, a short dumpling with a face as round as Ruby's belly, came out of the building next door.

"My Laud!" she cried and ran down the steps. "Freda! What happened to you?"

"That man followed us home." Freda pointed to Mr. Milton.

"Ruby Shade, what's going on? Who's that man?" Mrs. Johnson asked as she placed her arm around Freda and helped her walk to their gray stone building.

Neither Ruby nor Mr. Milton acknowledged the woman. They stared at each other. His pale eyes looked from her face to her big belly. Ruby shivered and crossed her arms. She instinctively stepped back.

"I'm calling the police," Mrs. Johnson yelled as she helped her daughter up the steps.

"You better go," Ruby said. Her gray eyes darkened with fear, and her lips trembled.

Out of the corner of her eye, Ruby saw the curtain at the living room window move. She knew Neecey was standing in the window, but she did not turn around or acknowledge her presence. Mr. Milton moved toward the window. Ruby jerked the sleeve of his coat and forced him to face her.

"What do you want?" she asked.

"Yo' auntie told me about the baby." Mr. Milton looked from Neecey to Ruby. "She gave me pictures. I watched my baby grow up in pictures."

"That baby died," Ruby lied. She rubbed the goose bumps on her arms.

"Naw," he shook his head. "Faith gave me the picture you sent. I saw my mama in her face."

"Why did I listen to Jesse?" Ruby said. "I shoulda never sent Aunt Faith pictures."

"You never sent yo' address before," Mr. Milton said. "Until this time."

He reached in his pocket and brought out a crumpled envelope. Ruby saw her own familiar block print across the center of the envelope. Then she saw Jesse's tight writing in the upper left-hand corner. She had asked him to mail the letter, and he had put the return address on the envelope.

She moved away from Mr. Milton, walked to the ledge by the living room window, and sat down. She saw the neighbors shaking their heads and murmuring. Ruby could hear the phone ringing tonight, and all the neighbors filling Louise in on the disgraceful scene.

You're right, Louise, the neighbors would say. *She ain't nothing. Ain't good enough for Jesse.*

"I'm married, Mr. Milton," she said and waved her ring finger in his face. The small diamond sparkled before him. "I got a new husband and two more children and I'm having another baby. I've been married for over six years now."

"But we's married," he said.

"My lawyer sent you the papers!" Ruby hissed. "All you had to do was sign them and return them to him."

"You got young'uns back home that need you," he said as he rolled the hat around and around in his hands. "What about Chauncey, Faye, and Edna?"

"Hmph! I got children here," Ruby said.

"I know," Mr. Milton said quietly. "But Pamela needs her own brother and her own sisters."

"Her daddy"—Ruby emphasized the word "daddy"—"calls her Neecey. We all call her Neecey. She don't know nothing about you, Mr. Milton."

"Y'all coming home," Mr. Milton said in a trembling voice.

"No!" Ruby cried. "Ain't never going back to Mansdale!"

His hand turned up in supplication. In that gesture, she saw the dead-end road that lead directly to his home. She saw the long dead-end days of tending children, washing overalls, cooking, and mending, all under the disapproving eyes of her Aunt Faith.

"No!" she shouted. She placed her hand against his chest and shoved him. He stumbled back toward the stairs. He regained his balance and moved toward her. She edged away toward the door.

"Silly old goat, you ain't got nothing here," Ruby said.

"You deny me my child?" he asked. He pointed to Neecey standing in the window. "That's my blood."

"No! You ain't got a damn thing here," Ruby shouted.

"So, you throw all decency away. For what, Ruby?"

"Go back to Mississippi!" she shouted. "Stay away from us."

"Running away from home like a child," he said. "What for? To sang in some juke joint? But you ain't sangin' now. Are you? Pretending to be married, but you're still my wife"

"Shut up!" Ruby cried. "Just shut up."

Milton moved toward the door. "I'm taking my child."

"No!" Ruby cried and shoved him.

He stumbled, then regained his balance. He moved around Ruby. She shoved him again and he fell against the concrete windowsill. Neecey jumped back, and the lace curtains fell into place. Through the curtains, Neecey watched the old man rise. He looked through the curtains and met Neecey's eyes. She stepped farther back, but Mr. Milton caressed the screen.

"This is my blood," he said again.

Mr. Milton turned toward Ruby and pulled her to him. "You always been an ornery thing. Gotta have yo' way all the time. But you ain't keeping my girl from me."

Then, like the Lone Ranger, Hopalong Cassidy, or Roy Rogers, Jesse leaped up the steps and snatched Mr. Milton away from Ruby. Jesse was upon him, beating him. Pow! Pow! Pow! Heigh-ho, Silver! Jesse's brown fist smashed into the yellow skin and sank into the sagging jaw. Jesse's thick lips curled back over his straight teeth as he grabbed the man's collar. He slammed him into the stone wall. Neecey heard the impact of the man's body. Jesse held on to the man's collar and punched him in the face again. The man slumped against the wall.

Jesse pulled him from the wall and slammed him into the con-crete again.

"Don't kill him, Jesse!" Ruby cried as she tugged at his arm.

"Kill him, Daddy!" Neecey shouted. "Kill him!"

A siren wailed down the street. People stood on several porches and watched with interest. Mr. Milton's nose and lips were bloody, and his eyes were swollen and purple.

"Jesse!" Pete caught Jesse's arm. Jesse snatched his arm away, grabbed Mr. Milton by the collar, and lifted him. Pete wrapped his arms around Jesse's waist and pulled him away from Mr. Milton. Once released, Mr. Milton slumped to the ground.

"Who the hell are you? Messing with my wife on my porch!" Jesse asked.

"It's Mr. Milton," Ruby said in an effort to calm Jesse just as two policemen raced up the steps. Pete threw his hands up and stepped back. Jesse stared at the man crumpled on the porch.

Pete spent most of the evening at the police station getting Jesse out on bail. The women made do with a dinner of bologna, Pepsi-Cola, and slices of pound cake. Ruby's black chicken lay in the cast-iron skillet on the stove. Della and Louise tiptoed around Ruby. Although neither of them had been home, they had learned about the incident from Mrs. Johnson.

Ruby, who had changed into a pink and lilac flowered housedress, stood at the sink washing dishes. Jack and Odessa were asleep. Neecey, in pajamas, sat at the kitchen table with Della and Louise. She rolled bits of bread into pellets and lined them on the edge of the table. Louise sipped her Pepsi and twirled her cigarette. Della nibbled on the pound cake on her saucer.

"Neecey, stop playing with yo' food and eat it!" Louise snapped.

"I hope they get back soon," Della said. "It's almost nine o'clock."

"Be damn lucky if they let Jess out tonight," Louise said. She took a drag from her cigarette and narrowed her eyes at Ruby's back.

Neecey opened her sandwich, lifted the bologna off the bread, and licked the mayonnaise. She rolled the bologna up and took a small bite from it.

"Mama, who was that man?" she asked.

Expectantly, Neecey and the women looked at Ruby scrubbing the counter. They waited for Ruby's answer, but she never turned. Louise looked at Della and frowned. Della shook her head.

"Mama," Neecey repeated, "who was that man?"

"Nobody, girl." Ruby tossed the answer over her shoulder without meeting Neecey's eyes or the eyes of the women.

"My daddy's Jesse, Mama?"

"Don't talk foolishness," Ruby said.

"Who's Chancey, Mama?"

"Chauncey," Louise corrected and twirled her glass of Pepsi. The click-click of the ice filled the small space of silence.

"And Edda?" Neecey asked.

"Edna," Louise corrected and took a sip from her glass as Della shook her head disapprovingly.

"And Faye?" Neecey asked.

Ruby remained silent. The ticking of the clock on the wall and the fizzing from Louise's Pepsi filled the silence. Della picked the crust from the pound cake.

"Mama," Neecey said after a pause, "who's they? Why did that man say he's my daddy?"

"Oh, damn!" Ruby shouted. She tossed the dish towel on the counter and fled from the kitchen.

"Those children are yo' brother and sisters," Louise said.

"Louise, don't."

"Well, somebody gotta tell the child about her family."

"That ain't yo' place," Della warned. "Jesse has said over and over that she belongs to him. He says that over and over. You better think before you say too much. Be a shame to lose a son over somebody you hate."

Neecey looked from Della's tight face to Louise's loose jowls. Louise shook her head and crammed her mouth with the remaining pound cake. Della reached across the table and stroked Neecey's face.

"Those are yo' brother and sisters, sweet pea," Della said. "But what do you call Jesse?"

"Daddy."

"And who takes you shopping?"

"Daddy."

"And who loves you?"

"Daddy."

"That's all you need to know, Neecey," Della said.

"Humph!" Louise said. Her massive body rose like a huge wave. She tugged her dress down and eased away from the table. "It's all gonna come out, sooner or later."

"That's all," Della reiterated. "That's all."

Neecey knew that was not all. Somewhere, there was a yellow bogeyman who had stolen Chauncey, Faye, and Edna, and who wanted to steal her too. Later that night, her sleep was disturbed by images of the yellow man with hazel eyes. He was

Rumpelstiltskin dancing before a huge fireplace. As he danced, he sang, *Hee, hee, hee. I come for my child. Hee, hee, hee.*

His green fish eyes spun in his skull like spinning tops. A stream of glitter shot from his eyes and swirled around the room. Neecey ran from the room, and the man ran behind her. His hard shoes echoed upon the sidewalks that opened and shut. She leapfrogged across the opening streets, but he was always one leap behind her. His huge shovel hand descended upon her shoulder. She woke up kicking and screaming.

"Nooooooo!"

Jesse gathered her in his arms. "It's okay, baby. It's okay."

"Daddy?"

"It's all right, buttercup," he said. "It's just a nightmare. Go back to sleep."

"Is that bogeyman gone?"

"Yeah, sweetie. He's gone," Jesse said. "You're safe."

She snuggled under the blanket. Jesse sat on the edge of the bed and stroked her temple. A sweet sleep came with no more thoughts of the bogeyman.

chapter 3

BIZARRO BALLAD

*g*ET OUT! Just get the hell out!" Ruby shouted.

Her voice traveled out the kitchen window that over-looked the balcony and reentered through the front door. She stormed around the small kitchen that sparkled with new white appliances. She slapped a dishcloth on the gray Formica table and scrubbed the surface with hard strokes. Four red-tufted back chairs circled around the table.

"You're putting all yo' business in the street," Jesse said from the living room. A large black Oriental breakfront separated the living room from the kitchen. Unruly ivy ran along the top of the breakfront while colorful glass and porcelain clowns danced across the shelves. Jesse lifted a dangling vine and placed it across the top of the breakfront.

"It's yo' business!" she said.

"You should have more pride."

Ruby slammed her hand on the table, braced herself, and turned her head toward him. The ceiling light caught the various hues of her red curls. He caught his breath. Even in anger, when her tiny lips disappeared and her gray eyes deepened to a charcoal color, she was breathtakingly beautiful. Before he could forget the argument and submerge himself in her beauty, profanity flew from her delicate lips.

"You can kiss my ass!" she hissed. The muscles in her face and throat hardened as she spoke. She turned to him, lifted one eyebrow, and spoke in a controlled voice. "You think you gonna stick me in the house with a bunch of babies while you run around? Hell, I coulda been on the road by now, singing. I coulda made a name for myself. I could be cutting records, but no, you got me stuck in the house with a bunch of damn babies while you run the streets."

"You got it all wrong," he said quietly as he closed and locked the front door next to the breakfront.

"Messing up my life while you ho around."

Ruby flung the dishcloth across the breakfront. It opened and blossomed, impotently hitting him in the chest. He turned and walked through the living room.

"Jesse, don't walk away from me!" Ruby called after him. "You tell that bitch not to call my house again!"

"Leave me alone, Ruby!" he shouted over his shoulder. "Leave me alone."

"Aaargh!" Ruby screamed and spun around in the kitchen. She grabbed a water glass, whirled, and threw it at Jesse's head. The glass shattered on the wall next to him and exploded in his ear. The glass shards popped into the back of his neck.

"Damn you!" he shouted and grabbed his neck. He pulled his hand away and looked at the red dots that covered his palm. He looked at her. "Ma'Dear is right. You're crazy. Crazy!"

"Crazy? She's the crazy one! Crazy and evil!" Ruby screamed.

He reached back and pulled one, two, four tiny shards from his neck. Jesse looked at her stomach and wondered if it would not be better for her to lose this child as she had lost the last one a year before. He wondered if he should place money in her hand and tell her, *Go, we'll be all right, Ruby. Go sing, dance, do whatever the hell you want!* He looked at the tiny woman moving slowly around the kitchen, cussing and waving her hand. Where was the soft, cuddly woman that he had married? Certainly, it was not this she-thing who cussed him like he was her enemy, not her husband. He turned and walked down the hall.

It was the breaking glass that woke nine-year-old Neecey. She sat up and squeezed into the corner of the bed. The cinder-block wall scratched one side of her back, while the sweaty tufted plastic of the Hollywood bed stuck against her arm. She wrapped her twiggy arms around her bony knees. The moonlight cascading through the window illuminated the room. In the dark, her familiar things contorted into frightful images. She thought she saw Boris Karloff standing in her closet. She looked again and saw it was only her bathrobe on a hook. She thought she saw a line of girls with missing legs. She looked again and saw only her dresses on hangers. She thought she saw the blockhead of Superman's alter ego, Bizarro. She looked again and saw only her stack of DC comic books.

"My auntie didn't raise no fool!" Ruby shouted.

Six-year-old Jack stirred and mumbled. Neecey quickly left her bed and kneeled before his. She rubbed his back gently. His breathing deepened. She wiped the sweat from his brow and his bushy eyebrows. A few drops of sweat on his thick curly lashes sparkled in the moonlight. On the other side of Jack, four-year-old Odessa slept peacefully with her thumb in her mouth. Neecey longed to curl up and snore, to sleep again, to sleep beyond the fight.

She wondered if Annette, Darlene, and Jimmy had received her letters. She had written to most of the Mouseketeers and told them how she could sing and dance and wanted to be the next Mouseketeer. She would fly to Disneyland and get her own special shirt with her name, *Neecey,* across her chest. No more fights. *M-I-C, see you real soon. K-E-Y, why, because we like you.* And all the Mouseketeers would like her. She would be the first Negro on *The Mickey Mouse Club.*

She returned to her bed and kneeled in the window. She watched the North-South el rattle along its tracks. The red neon lights of Stateway Liquors blinked off and on. The muted sound of late-night traffic and the heavy hot stench from the Chicago stockyards drifted into the open window.

For almost a year, Neecey had wallowed in the luxury of her own room, and it didn't matter that she had to share it with Jack and Odessa. She had a twin-size bed all to herself. For a year, her home, her life, had been just as comfortable as Princess's on the television show *Father Knows Best.* For almost a year, the family had enjoyed the beauty of the gleaming white Stateway Gardens housing development. Showy red geraniums and luscious velvet grass surrounded the development. For a year, the family had enjoyed the convenience of living a block from Thirty-fifth and State. A short walk east and they could watch a slew of cartoons and a double feature at the Louis Theater for a quarter. A short walk west and they could enjoy the Chicago White Sox clobbering a visiting team inside Comiskey Park.

Then, after one year of happiness in their new apartment, *the ho* had intruded into their lives. Invisibly, she sat at the dinner table, walked the halls, and dragged Jesse away for days at a time. Neecey had never seen *the ho,* but she knew her name—Gwen. Gwen had sucked the happiness from the pores of their new glossy concrete walls.

"You ain't gonna make a fool out of me!" Ruby screamed.

"I see the moon, and the moon sees me," Neecey recited, looking up at the hazy full moon. She stuck her fingers in her ears and clicked her teeth together. Still, Ruby's thunderous words crashed through Neecey's door.

"You gonna wake the kids," Jesse said from outside Neecey's bedroom door.

His footsteps broke the slant of light underneath her door as he walked to the bathroom. Neecey followed Jesse's movements by the sound he made: Water splashed into the sink. The medicine cabinet whined open. The bottles and jars clattered together.

"You don't give a damn 'bout those kids!" Ruby yelled.

Inside the bathroom, Jesse removed a bottle of Mercurochrome and a box of cotton from the medicine cabinet. He soaked the cotton with Mercurochrome, then dabbed it on his neck. In the bathroom mirror, he watched Ruby move into the dim light of the hallway.

Unthinkingly he asked, "Any aspirin?"

"I'm the one with the headache!" Ruby yelled as she stepped inside the bathroom. "I'm the one stuck in this damn apartment while you're screwing yo' ho!"

"You gonna wake the kids with this mess," Jesse said quietly.

"Mess!" Ruby shouted. "You started this mess!"

"Ruby, leave me alone," Jesse said.

"I'll kill you!" Ruby screamed and charged into Jesse.

He fell against the sink and hit his head against the mirror. The mirror shattered. The bottle of Mercurochrome fell from his hand and ran like blood down the sink and into the drain. His headache and the pain from hitting the mirror married and, for a moment, that union blinded him. He twisted around and grabbed Ruby's hands.

"Turn me loose, Jesse!" she screamed hysterically as she tried to get out of his grip. That scream roused Odessa, who sat up and wailed. That wail woke Jack with a start.

"Mama!" Jack cried.

Neecey jumped into the bed with them. Odessa scrambled into Neecey's arm and buried her face in Neecey's neck. Like she had done so many times before, Neecey wrapped her left arm around Jack.

"No, Jack! Stay here!" Neecey tightened her grip around him.

"I want my mama!" Jack cried and struggled against Neecey.

"You think you gonna trap me with a bunch of babies while you run the streets?" Ruby screamed.

"Shirley Temple went to France," Neecey sang, "to teach the girls the Watusi dance."

"You got the kids upset," Jesse said.

"First on the heel, then on the toe," Neecey recited. "Round and around and around she goes."

"When you turn me loose, I'm gonna slice you to kingdom come," Ruby cried.

"Salute to the captain. Bow to the queen. Search the sky for a special dream."

"You're acting like one of those heifers on the street," Jesse said.

"You're not gonna walk all over me!" Ruby screamed. "I don't need you! I don't need this shit!"

Neecey's gown soaked up Jack and Odessa's tears and mucus. Suddenly, everything was still and quiet outside the bedroom door. Neecey's heart beat fast. She heard it in her head. She felt a dry heat in her mouth. Another el rattled across the tracks. In the distance, the wail of a fire truck surged toward the building. The curtains fluttered at the window, and the sweet stench from the stockyards whizzed around their heads. Odessa lifted her face from Neecey's neck and scooted down into the crook of Neecey's arm.

"Jesse, turn me loose," Ruby's voice crackled. She beat her hands against his chest and kicked at his legs.

"When you calm down," Jesse promised.

"You can't hold me forever," Ruby said.

"You need to stop this foolishness," Jesse said.

"Foolishness!" Ruby shouted.

"Ruby, stop before you hurt yourself," he cooed, hoping to calm her down.

Yet his voice did not calm her. She shoved and pushed until they crashed into the bathroom door and fell back into the hall. He had no choice but to release her. The moment Jesse released her, Ruby charged into him again. He fell against the children's door. The door banged against the wall. Neecey jumped. Jack took advantage of the moment to leap out of the bed.

"Mama! Mama!" he cried.

Ruby charged into Jesse yet again. He stumbled but managed to grab her. She reached up and clawed his face.

"Damn!" Jesse yelled and released her.

Ruby flew into him and grabbed another hunk of flesh. Blood flowed down his cheeks. Jesse managed to capture her hands. She struggled against him. She tried to raise her knee to his groin, but he jumped back. He maneuvered his body until he was behind her. Ruby twisted and turned in his grasp, but she could not break his grip. Jesse glanced at Jack, who stood in the center of the bedroom wailing, and then at Neecey, who still cuddled Odessa.

"Ruby, you don't want the children to see us act like this. Let's go back to the front."

"Imma catch you with her and it's gonna be over, Jesse. It's gonna be over," Ruby said.

"You know I love you," Jesse said.

"What you know 'bout love is less than the last line of a matchbook cover," she snarled.

"Ruby, let's stop this for the children," Jesse pleaded. "For them."

Ruby looked at the crying children. Then, tired of fighting, tired of him, she slumped in Jesse's arms. He released her, and she walked out the room.

"It's okay, y'all. It's okay," Jesse said. "Jack, go back to bed, son. Everything is fine."

"Daddy?" Neecey cried.

"Get back in yo' own bed, Neecey," Jesse said. "It'll be all right by morning." He tucked the children in bed and kissed them good night.

THE HOT ODOR from the stockyards rose like steam. A brilliant, white-hot sun burned all the blue from the sky. Ruby led her brood to the bus stop. Her tawny red hair sparkled in the sunlight. Her green maternity top billowed over her stomach. She carried a gray quart-size thermos under one arm. Her pocketbook dangled from the other arm. Neecey and Odessa trailed behind her in stiff pink dresses. Jack, jaunting ahead of them, wore a holster around his waist. He pointed his cap gun at the passing cars and shouted, "Bang! Bang!"

Ruby, the children, and the bus made it to the corner simultaneously. The stench from the stockyards was omnipresent, like skin on the body—always there. The putridly sweet odor of burning cow and pig blood and guts blew into every open window of the 36A State Street bus as it made its way south. Soon the bus eased into the heavenly aroma of freshly baked bread that drifted from the commercial bakery on Fifty-fifth and State.

The family changed buses on Fifty-ninth Street and rode over to Peoria. The street was deserted. Most of the black residents of Englewood were lined up along the two-mile stretch on South Park, watching the Bud Billiken Parade. On the second Saturday of every August, the majority of Chicago's black community flocked to the parade for a chance to see Roy Rogers and his horse, Trigger, Hopalong Cassidy, Joe Louis, or Lena Horne. At Louise's, Ruby set the children in the shade of the porch.

"Don't move," she said, "don't move an inch."

The children sat there, afraid of the tightness in their mother's voice, afraid of her granite gray eyes. The threat was tiny and invisible, but each felt it cutting into them, choking them into silence. Neecey clutched the purse that Ruby shoved into her hands. Ruby tucked the thermos under her arm, inserted a key into the lock, and entered the vestibule.

She eased open the door of the apartment. From the kitchen came the sound of pots and pans, running water, and china. The smell of bacon and baking biscuits drifted through the house. Ruby eased the door closed and scurried behind the jungle of plants. She peered through a few leaves. The door to her old bedroom was closed, but she heard Jesse's booming laughter followed by the small giggling of a woman.

"Stop, Jesse! Stop!"

Ruby unscrewed the thermos and the strong odor of gasoline hit her nose. Her stomach heaved and fell. She turned her head and breathed. She held her face in her armpit and sniffed the clean scent of Dial soap and Ban deodorant.

Through the gilded mirror in the hall, she watched Louise

move around the kitchen. Louise poured coffee into her best china server. She returned the coffeepot to the stove and lifted the tray. A crooked smile was on her moon face as she gingerly carried the tray out of the kitchen and down the hall. She softly knocked on the closed door.

"Jesse?" she called, all soft and apologetic. "Jesse, I done fixed y'all some breakfast."

"Yeah, Ma'Dear," he answered.

Ruby felt as if one of the vines from the plant had wrapped around her neck. She tried to catch her breath, but it came in short snatches. Jesse's child flip-flopped in her womb. She was conscious of floating down a river of death. Inside the room, Gwen, a tiny woman with a mop of coarse hair, laid upon the pillows that Ruby had once slept on. Jesse was the first to see Ruby.

"Oh, shit!" he exclaimed and leaped from the bed.

He held a pillow before his manhood like every woman in that room had not seen him naked at some time in his life. Louise, pouring coffee into a cup, caught sight of Ruby in the dresser mirror. She trembled so hard that the cup and saucer rattled like windows in a tornado. She set everything down and slowly turned.

"What the hell are you doing here?" Gwen screamed and pulled the sheet up to her little pointy chin.

"Ruby, now don't go to pieces," Jesse pleaded.

His words brought Ruby out of her fog. She walked up to the bed and yanked the sheet out of Gwen's hand. Gwen squirmed and tried to cover her nakedness. Before any of them knew her intentions, Ruby dashed the gasoline on her. Gwen screamed as gasoline popped into her eyes. She sputtered as it flowed from her lower face and mouth, down her body. Ruby flung the thermos on the bed and grabbed Gwen's hair. She dragged the screaming woman from the bed.

"What the hell are you doing?" Louise screamed and rushed toward Ruby. Then she saw the butane lighter in Ruby's hand.

"Come on, old crow," Ruby snarled. "Come on and we'll all burn in hell."

"Jesse!" Gwen cried and rubbed her eye, but that only made the icy pain worse.

"She's crazy," Louise said, and stepped back.

"Now, Ruby, baby," Jesse stuttered. His eyes never left Ruby's finger on the flint as he moved his foot around on the floor, searching for his pants. All she had to do was flick the flint and the gasoline would ignite.

"Yeah, you like fish," Ruby teased Jesse. "We're gonna have a good fish-fry."

Gwen sputtered as the taste of gasoline washed her mouth. The gasoline clouded her sight. She rubbed her eyes. They continued to burn. She tried to pull away from Ruby. Then she felt the cold square-shaped metal on her skin. The odor from the flint reinforced what she already knew: Ruby had a lighter.

"Why you wanna come in my house with all this shit!" Louise asked.

"Ma'Dear, shut up!" Jesse said.

"She don't scare me!" Louise said.

"Ma'Dear, you stay out of this!" Jesse screamed. "You stay out of it."

"Jesse," Gwen whimpered.

"You should have told her that when she was serving you breakfast in bed," Ruby said. Her voice was calm. Her movements were slow, serene, and alert. Ruby walked backward and tugged Gwen out of the bedroom by her hair.

"Where's my damn pants?" Jesse cried.

Gwen wept, fearful halting sobs with strange little hiccups —*eeheecup, eeheecup*.

At the front door, Ruby's position became perilous. She could not release Gwen's hair and open the door, nor could she open the door with the hand that held the lighter. Ruby watched as Jesse stepped into his pants. She had a moment to decide.

"It don't matter to me," she said to Gwen, "who dies today."

"What?" Gwen asked, but she heard the fatality in Ruby's voice.

"Open the door," Ruby said.

"Ain't got no clothes on," Gwen cried.

"My arm might get burned, but your face will be burnt to a crisp, if you don't open that door," Ruby said and moved the lighter before Gwen's eyes.

Gwen opened the door, and Ruby led her into the vestibule. Through the glass door, Gwen saw the bright day and knew she could not face the world naked.

"Ruby, please, I ain't got no clothes on. Please."

"You ain't begged me for my husband. Open it."

NEECEY SAT IN THE SHADE of Louise's building and hissed *stop* every time Jack shot his cap gun. Sweat glistened on her face. She imagined a tall glass of milk with Bosco chocolate syrup. She imagined a tall glass of grape Kool-Aid with slices of lemon. She imagined a plain glass of ice water. Her tongue was thick and heavy with thirst. She opened Ruby's handbag and searched for the customary pack of Juicy Fruit gum.

"I want some wada," Odessa whined as she pushed against Neecey's leg.

"We gotta wait for Mama," Neecey said as she swallowed to wet her parched throat. She found the familiar yellow pack and removed three sticks of gum.

"I'll go get her," Jack said and jumped down.

"You gonna get us in trouble," Neecey said as she stuck a piece of gum in Odessa's mouth.

"Trouble! Trouble!" Jack shouted. "This is what I'll do to trouble!" He whipped his cap gun from its holster. "Bang! Bang! Bang!"

"Sit down and be quiet, Jack," she ordered, handing him a piece of gum.

Just then the vestibule door opened, and the gum was forgotten. The gun fell from Jack's hand, and Neecey's eyes widened as Ruby and Gwen emerged from the building. Ruby marched boldly out of the house with her head high and a grin on her face. Gwen wrapped her arms around her breasts and her upper thighs. She tried to bend forward, but Ruby yanked her hair back.

"She's buck naked," Jack exclaimed.

"Hush up, boy, and sit yo butt down," Ruby said. She yanked Gwen past the children.

"Jesse!" Gwen screamed. She tried to twist her legs together, to hide herself with her small hands.

Ruby put her mouth close to Gwen's ear and hissed, "Don't you get it? You ain't nothing but a piece of tail."

Ruby shoved the naked woman onto Jesse's black Impala. The woman danced in front of the car as she tried to cover her breasts and privates. She stooped to her haunches and tried to hide herself from the stares of the people.

Moments before, Peoria Street had been empty, quiet.

Now, a man two doors down rose from his stoop to watch the naked woman dance. A couple of teenage boys rode by on their bikes and crashed into parked cars. Across the street, a woman in a straw hat peeped over her hedges.

The door opened again, and Louise stepped from the building. "You're humiliating me!" she cried.

"You didn't think about my shame," Ruby said.

"Ma'Dear," Jack cried as he ran to her.

"You got these kids watching this mess!" Louise screamed as she struggled to lift six-year-old Jack. She walked to the edge of the steps. "What kinda woman are you?"

Odessa pressed against Neecey. Neecey pulled her closer. A hot flush ran through Neecey. Grown-ups' fussing was scarier than the Werewolf or Frankenstein. Grown-ups' fussing was like being left alone in the dark. Neecey trembled as Louise's shadow fell over them.

"Don't you talk to me about decency!" Ruby barked.

"You're fighting over a man that don't want you," Louise said.

"This ain't about him wanting me," Ruby said. "It's about Gwen and me. Gwen coulda slept with him on top of the Prudential Building for all I cared. But she brought her skinny ass up to my apartment and pretended she was at the wrong door."

"Gwen!" Jesse called from the doorway.

He walked next to Louise and threw an orange and white polka-dot dress toward Gwen. The dress billowed and sailed like a kite. Ruby grabbed the dress before it landed on the sidewalk between her and the woman.

"She's a ho," Ruby stated. "She don't need clothes."

"Daddy!" Odessa ran to him and grabbed his leg.

"Ruby, why you got these kids here?" he asked as he lifted Odessa.

"Who the hell gonna take care of yo' children while you're screwing around?"

"Ruby . . ."

"Don't Ruby me!" she screamed. "You got down on yo' knees and swore that you love me. Did you know that, silly girl? You calling me, saying 'Jesse don't want you. He loves me.' You think I'm some stupid woman trying to hold on to a cheating man. Hell, naw! All he gotta do is take his damn kids and get out of my life."

A siren wailed in the distance. The watching people no longer pretended to be busy. They inched closer to the scene. One of the boys on the bikes laughed at Gwen dancing on her haunches beside the car.

"Give her the dress, Ruby," Jesse said as he adjusted Odessa in his arm.

"Go to hell," she said. Ruby crumpled the dress into a ball and tucked it under her arm. "Neecey, come with me."

Neecey scooped up Ruby's pocketbook from the concrete ledge and slung it over her shoulder. She squeezed the gum in her hand.

"Ruby, the police are coming," Jesse said.

"I ain't the one dancing naked in the street," Ruby said.

"Just give her the damn dress," he said.

"Humph!" Ruby snorted, grabbed Neecey's arm, and started down Peoria toward Sixty-third Street.

"What about the kids?" Louise said.

"You such a good madam," Ruby said. "You watch 'em."

PREMATURELY, Ruby gave birth to Serenda Joy the third week of August. Jesse and Neecey cleaned the apartment thoroughly, while Jack and Odessa dabbed at dusting furniture.

Laughter rebounded off the walls and drifted out the open door.

"Serenda Joy," Jesse sang as he slung the mop across the linoleum floors.

"Is she pretty, Daddy?" Neecey asked as she washed dishes.

"She's a real doll." He laughed.

"When we gonna get another brother?" Jack asked.

"Maybe soon," Jesse laughed.

Whatever plans Jesse had to increase the family disappeared three weeks after Ruby's homecoming. One day after school, Odessa and Serenda's cries greeted Neecey and Jack as they entered the apartment. The apartment was ominously dark. All the shades were lowered and the drapes drawn. Odessa, with mucus and tears running down her face, ran to Neecey. Ruby, wrapped in her white chenille robe, sat on the sofa with her hair in kit curlers. Her eyes were red and swollen.

"You all right, Mama?" Neecey asked as she stroked Odessa's hair.

"The baby is crying," Ruby said and closed her eyes.

"Mama?" Neecey asked.

"Get the baby, Neecey. Get the baby."

"Mama?" Jack questioned. He walked up to her and touched her face. Ruby looked into his caramel eyes with thick black lashes and heavy eyebrows.

"Oh, Jesse! Jesse!" she sobbed and gathered Jack into her arms.

chapter 4

BEGGAR'S TIMBRE

*t*HE APARTMENT was no longer bright but dark and heavy with loneliness, Ruby's and the children's. Jesse was not there to tumble the children out of bed, to carry them piggyback through the apartment, nor to fix them bowls of corn flakes. He was not there to laugh at *Mighty Mouse* on Saturday mornings, nor to explain *Sky King* on Saturday afternoons. He was not there to teach them to ride a bike, fly a kite, or utter parental platitudes that always irritated but lingered long into a child's old age.

"Mama, where's Daddy?" Jack asked.

"Boy, get out my face!" Ruby barked.

"Mama, when's Daddy coming home?" Neecey asked.

"Don't ask me no damn questions about that man!"

Unexpectedly, Jesse would drop by with bags of food and toys. He wrestled with Jack on the floor, helped Neecey with schoolwork, tossed Odessa in the air, and cuddled Serenda. Yet these visits were erratic and all so short. Too soon, he grabbed his hat and headed for the door. The children wept and pleaded, *Don't go, Daddy. Don't go.* Yet Ruby was unforgiving, and when Jesse looked at her with pleading eyes, she turned her head. Jesse's visits became fewer and farther apart.

One winter afternoon, Neecey sat at the kitchen table

sipping hot Ovaltine while Ruby peeled sweet potatoes. The kitchen was warm with the aroma of baking corn bread and frying pork chops. Neecey kicked her legs, sipped the Ovaltine, and watched snow whirl outside the window. As far as she could see, the world was a ballroom of dancing snow. The snow had slowed life to a crawl, so she was surprised to see Della trudging across the balcony.

"Here comes Auntie Della," she said to Ruby.

"Laud, why's she out in this weather? Door's open, Della!" Ruby called.

The breakfront shielded Neecey's back from the blast of cold air that came through the door with Della. Della quickly closed the door and placed her pocketbook on the breakfront.

"It's a mess out there," she said and began peeling off her outwear.

"Della, did you drive through that mess?" Ruby asked.

"Naw, girl. Pete dropped me off," she said and draped her coat on the coat rack next to the door. "He had a run to make on the West Side. Crazy man! You can barely see the roads out there."

"Hi, Auntie!" Neecey called.

"Hi, sugar. Where're the other little noisemakers?"

"They're sleeping," Neecey said.

"There's a little hot milk on the stove, Della. Make yourself some Ovaltine."

Della got a cup from the dish rack and squeezed past Ruby to the stove. The kitchen was a small affair. Ruby had added colorful ceramic canisters, novelty salt and pepper shakers, and a string of colorful handmade potholders to add warmth to the white steel cabinets and white appliances. However, since the table and four red vinyl chairs swallowed up most of the room, her added touches gave the kitchen a cluttered appearance. On the rare occasions that Ruby and the children ate together, the five of them jammed into that small space like bulls in a box. Bedlam drove that small room. The children raced for chairs and, in their hungry glee, swung their legs back and forth under the table.

"You kicked me," one child would say to another.

"No, I didn't," the other child would reply.

"Yes, you did."

Licks would pass and anger would rise until Ruby slammed a bowl on the table and ordered, "Stop that shit!"

Food sloshed from the bowl to the table and the children looked accusingly one another.

"You did it!"

"No, you did it!"

Della placed two heaping tablespoons of Ovaltine in the cup and stirred in the hot milk.

"What's going on, Della?" Ruby asked as Della sat down.

"Nothing," Della answered and nervously twirled her cup. She squinted her small eyes. A nervous tick appeared at the corner of her mouth. She scratched her right eyebrow, held her cheek, and gave a small shake to her head. Ruby continued slicing the sweet potatoes. Della leaned to the side and pulled an envelope from her pocket. She pushed the envelope toward Ruby.

"What's that?" Ruby asked.

"That's from Jesse."

"What? He's sending his few dollars by you now? He can't come by and see his children?"

"Neecey, honey, go watch television or something," Della said. "Is it all right if she takes her Ovaltine?"

"Go on, Neecey. Watch television," Ruby said.

Neecey picked up her cup and eased out of her chair and

around the breakfront. She turned the television to *Dennis the Menace,* which she didn't like and had no intention of watching. She positioned herself at the end of the sofa so she could have a partial view of the kitchen.

"Go on, Della," Ruby urged, "spill it."

"Jesse can't come by right now, Ruby. He's out of town."

Only the sizzle of pork chops and the ticking of the cat clock on the wall filled the kitchen with sound. Ruby looked at Della. Della was not a liar. Still, Ruby knew there was more to that envelope. She rose from the table and lifted the bowl of sweet potatoes.

"What else, Della?"

"He's selling dope."

"Damn!" Ruby exclaimed. "Jesse and those stupid reefers."

She rinsed the sweet potatoes, placed them in a pot, and covered them with sugar and butter. After the potatoes were placed over a low fire, she removed golden brown pork chops from the cast-iron skillet. Ruby sensed something foreboding—an emptiness that she could not fill. She lifted a fork of greens from the pot on the back burner and gingerly tasted them. She added a dash of crushed red pepper. Using a dish towel, she removed the pan of corn bread from the oven. Della nervously fidgeted with the cup. Something scary itched in Ruby's mind. Something she knew and didn't know. Della looked like a nervous thief. There was more to the story than selling reefers.

Ruby turned to Della. Neecey quickly averted her eyes back to the television. She hated television shows with no pretty women, and all the women on *Dennis the Menace* were plain—not like the gorgeous Loretta Young or the pretty Ann Sheridan.

"What else, Della?" Ruby asked.

"I think he's hooked," Della said.

"Girl, Jesse says you can't get hooked on reefers."

"I think Jesse's beyond reefers," Della said.

"What are you telling me?"

"I'm talking horse, Ruby."

"Horse?"

"Heroin."

"No, Jesse ain't crazy." Ruby shook her head as she eased into her chair and lifted the envelope. Money spilled onto the table. "Shit!"

Neecey drained her cup, stood up, and walked into the kitchen. Her eyes fell on the bills in the center of the table. Ruby quickly stuffed the money back into the envelope.

"I told you to watch TV."

"I gotta put my cup in the sink," Neecey said.

The women were quiet until Neecey was again in front of the television.

"Dope?" Ruby gestured with the envelope.

"Dope." Della nodded.

It became a habit for Neecey to catch snippets of hush-hush conversations between Della and Ruby. Once she heard:

Della: He got ten years, Louise told us.

Ruby: Spoiled the man. That's why he's in this jam.

Another time, it was:

Della: I hate that Jesse left you in a bind.

Ruby: If it wasn't for Aunt Faith, me and these kids would be out on the street.

Those snippets revealed Louise's new marriage and move to Peoria and Pete and Della's new home in Chatham. Those snippets, she felt, held the key to Jesse's disappearance.

SOMETHING INSIDIOUS slithered into the apartment. Hunger. Hunger crept into their lives like a mist—fine, invisible, increasing until it could not be hidden. First came days and days of potatoes: fried for breakfast, french fried for lunch, boiled for dinner. A spell of spaghetti followed the potatoes. A multitude of beans swept away the spaghetti: red beans, navy beans, lima beans, and pinto beans. When the beans vanished, bread wandered into the apartment and stayed: toast for breakfast, peanut-butter sandwiches for lunch and dinner, and mayonnaise-and-sugar sandwiches before bed. Always with each meal came the bland, opaque, nonfat dry milk with lumps.

Neecey spent the ninth winter of her life traveling around the building begging for Ruby. Ruby might sit in some woman's kitchen and casually ask, "Girl, you got a cup of sugar I can borrow?" but she would never directly ask them for money. She could not bear the humiliation of begging for coins. So, she sent Neecey.

Miz Myrtle, my mama say would you lend her fifty cents?

Miz Erma, my mama say would you lend her a quarter?

Miz Betty, my mama say would you lend her a dollar?

While she waited for the women to dig into their pocketbooks for the precious coins, Neecey held her head down, scuffled her shoes along the floor, and hoped her classmates would not recognize her. Inadvertently one would, and the next day Neecey would be the butt of *yo' mama* jokes.

Hey, Neecey! Yo mama so po' she serves strings for spaghetti.

Hey, Neecey! Yo mama so po' she and the rats have tug-of-war over bread.

Taunts and teases she survived, and even irregular meals. It would take a while, but she would learn to do without. Later, as an adult, she would eat one tiny meal a day and feel stuffed. For now, she ate tiny morsels and passed the remainder of her food to Jack, Odessa, or Serenda. Any who needed or wanted more. Although both Jesse and his envelopes of money had disappeared, there were days that money appeared in envelopes from Mississippi, and then the family feasted. It was on such a day during the summer of her tenth birthday that Neecey skipped out of her apartment with two quarters clutched in her fingers for Edith Strickland. That summer day held promise. For once, her belly was full and she was child-free. Jack and Odessa were spending the weekend with Louise. Neecey, her hair freshly washed and pressed, a crisp new shorts outfit on, and a nickel in her pocket, would swing in the big playground. She would jump double Dutch with Marie and Sheila. She would spend her nickel on a cherry snowball.

Neecey skipped through the vestibule to the other side of the floor. She knocked rapidly on Edith's door. There was no sound. She knocked again. Yells and shouts of children at play drifted up from the playground below. A happy rumble came from the el tracks. Traffic whistled by, and Neecey impatiently leaned against the wall next to the door. A muffled shuffle came from within, but no one answered the door. Neecey turned to leave, and the door swung open.

"Yeah?"

Booker, Edith's heavyset, balding husband, barked at her. The big toe on his right foot poked through a hole in his sock. His blue work pants were stained with motor oil. His white undershirt had food stains and handprints. His round eyes were bloodshot. Sweat ran from his bumpy brow down his pockmarked face and into the fat folds of his neck.

"Is Miz Edith home?" Neecey asked.

"Whadya want with her?" he slurred.

"My mama told me to give her this." Neecey held the money out to him.

Booker leered at the two quarters in her hand. He didn't take the quarters nor inform Neecey if Edith was home or not. He looked at the quarters, then at her face. Another el rumbled by, but he said nothing. Then he stepped back and opened the door.

"Come on in," he said and smiled.

Neecey noticed that one of his side teeth was missing. She walked into the apartment. He slammed the door and twisted the lock. She stood in the middle of the floor and waited for him to call Edith. Instead, he eyed her up and down.

"You look really pretty today," he said. "Why you so dolled up? You got a boyfriend?"

"No, sir," she answered, "I just gotta give Mrs. Strickland this money."

"Pretty thang like you," he said and tugged one of her glossy braids. "Gotta have a boyfriend."

She backed away from him. Suddenly the apartment was too dark, too ominous, like the Haunted House at Riverview Amusement Park. His face was like one of those that jumped out of the darkness. He was too close and smelled bad—a nasty smell like the whiskey and beer smell when her daddy used to come home too late.

"Don't you like boys?" he asked as he stroked her hair.

She backed away from him. Now she was on the fastest roller coaster—*The Bob*. She was plunging straight to death.

"I gotta go." She handed him the coins.

He clasped his big bear paws around her skinny chicken fingers and pulled her to him. He kneeled before her. He took the quarters from her and shoved them into the pocket of her shorts. His fingers kneaded her thigh inside the pocket. She pushed at his arms. He tugged her pocket and pulled her against his chest.

"I gotta go," she said again, clawing at his arm.

"Don't," he said and pulled her to him. He licked her face. She grimaced and swiped the saliva from her face.

"Stop! Leave me alone," she cried and struggled to get away from his hands.

He snatched her hands, imprisoned them in his, and pulled her to him. His hot breath hit her face. "I don't want to hurt you," he said. "I just want to love you."

She struggled as he lifted her. Her feet and legs flailed against his body as she struggled to get out of his arms.

"Turn me loose!" she screamed. He held her against his body with one arm and clasped his free hand over her mouth. She clawed at his hands, at his face, kicking against him. He was impervious to her action. All the porous holes in the cinder-block wall were eyes, just watching as he carried her through the house to his bedroom. With his mouth close to her ear, he whispered, "It's okay, girl."

In the bedroom, he dumped her on the bed, and she bounced. She scrambled to get away from him. He grabbed her hair and slung her back onto the bed.

"Don't," he said. "I don't want to hurt you, but I will. I will hurt you bad."

He looked down at her and she was afraid in her stomach, in her chest. She sucked the air. Breathing was hard. She felt him, from far away, unbuttoning her blouse. She slapped at his hands. He pressed his hand against her throat.

"Do you want to die?" he asked.

She shook her head.

"Then lay still."

She held her head back and looked up and out the window.

The sky was pale blue with fluffy white clouds. She heard the laughter of children and traffic. The world was still out there, away from him. She felt his hands tugging her shorts down. She felt his hand down there. She turned her head and squeezed her eyes shut. He was on her heavy, bricks, walls, ceilings, sky, on her. The sourness of his breath and the funkiness of his body smothered her. She should die. She should die.

The moment passed in a blur of pain, traffic noises, and children's voices. Passed until she was sitting in the stairwell. She heard his voice in her head, *Tell somebody and I'll kill you.* She wondered why her legs hurt, why she wanted to crawl into the garbage chute and fall down into the fiery incinerator. Years later, when she rode the North-South el past Stateway Gardens, her mouth would curl in disgust.

chapter 5

ROCK

*N*EECEY SPOTTED BOOKER standing on the corner of Thirty-sixth and State. His balding head gleamed above those of the other men. Unemployed men, night shift men, or men in passing who congregated in front of the liquor store. They whistled at women, slapped skin, tipped bottles, and spoke above the roar of the North-South el. They lied and dreamed, found comfort in each other's company. Some walked away with a little more hope. Others lingered, afraid to return to the bleakness of their lives.

Spotting Booker's head, Neecey blended into the crowd of schoolchildren and rushed across the street with them. She raced into the lobby of her building. Unlike the other children, she didn't laugh or joke but stood before the elevator, pressing her books into her chest as her left leg shook. Her eyes shifted back and forth, from the light panel above the elevator door to the glass panes of the entrance doors.

Come on, she thought. *Hurry.*

The elevator door opened, and the children crowded on, shouting *Ouch, Don't push,* or *That's my foot.* Neecey forced her way to the back of the elevator. She breathed a sigh of relief and fell against the elevator wall.

Then in stepped Booker, reeking of liquor. He saw her at

the back of the elevator and squeezed through the children to get as close to her as possible. He ended up standing adjacent to her.

"Hey, Booker." A woman in a pink flowered dress squeezed into the last available space just before the door slithered closed.

The cables groaned as the elevator rose. The groan eased into a smooth whine. Booker nudged against Neecey. She squeezed closer to a boy with a greasy brown bag of potato chips.

"Girl, get off me," the boy said, and shoved her against Booker.

Neecey cringed and drew her arms tightly against her body. The elevator stopped on the second floor and three girls squeezed past the woman in the pink dress.

"Damn," the woman said. "You little heifers coulda walked up one flight."

Booker took advantage of the distraction to nudge against Neecey. His hand brushed her arm. A shiver, a minute movement, barely decipherable, coursed through her arm. He smirked and pinched her.

"What's Edith up to?" the woman asked.

"She at her mama's house today," he said. "Ed working yet?"

"No, he still waiting for Flavor-Kist to call him," she said. "What about you?"

Neecey wanted to climb over the laughing and teasing heads of the children and crawl through the roof of the elevator. She would scale the cables, then burst through the roof of the building, and soar through the sky until she was safe in Disneyland.

After more children relinquished space on the third and

fourth floors, Neecey moved from the back of the elevator to stand close to the door. Only Booker, the woman, three girls, and the boy with the potato chips were still on the elevator.

"Cinderella went to France," she hummed.

Two more floors and Booker would drag her into his apartment or onto the stairwell. On the next floor, the boy got off. Neecey heard the blood racing through her body. The boom-boom of her heart echoed like a voice in an empty room. Neecey dashed through the closing elevator doors before they clanged shut and saw the boy disappear through the swinging doors.

Booker was trapped with the woman and the girls for another floor—his floor, her floor. She could not go up. Neecey ran through the doorway next to the elevator. She slipped, and her books dropped to the floor. She retrieved them and dashed down the stairs. On the next floor she heard a door above her open onto the stairwell, and construction boots pounded down the stairs. She ran, jumped down the last two steps, and round the banister to the next flight of stairs. She ran and jumped, ran and jumped, while the pounding of the boots overhead merged with the hard pounding of her heart. Her legs ached, but she could not, dared not slow her pace. The distance between her and the boots shortened.

"Lobby, lobby, lobby," she muttered as she flew down and around, down and around. The lobby door was there, a short flight away. Neecey leaped, fell against the door, and landed on her knees in the lobby. A group of children laughed.

"Neecey, are you all right?" Sarah, Ruby's next-door neighbor, asked as she lifted her from the floor. Neecey could only cling to her arms and nod her head as the heavy footsteps faded behind the closing door. She had escaped one more time.

AS IF NEECEY'S LIFE wasn't bad enough with the constant dodging of Booker, Ruby took in a boarder named Keith. Keith was a tall yellow man with a flight of freckles across his cheeks and a nose shaped like a crookneck squash.

Keith stuffed his possessions into the walk-in closet and sprawled on the sofa. Neecey did not know where he came from and could not understand why he was there. How could Ruby allow him to sleep on the sofa when Jesse was out there somewhere? Neecey did not know that Keith's five dollars a week brought food for her and her siblings. She knew only the coil of fear that squatted on her chest when Keith wrestled with Jack, coochy-cooed Odessa and Serenda, and rustled Neecey's hair. That coil tightened when he looked at her and ran his tongue over his top lip. He stalked her like a panther, watching, brushing against her accidentally. She cringed and found Ruby's side the best place to be under his ogling eyes. Yet Ruby did not want the child under her.

"Neecey, get away from me," Ruby ordered and shoved her away.

Keith smirked. He pressed coins into Odessa's and Jack's hands and they giggled with anticipation of ice cream, candy, anything sweet on their tongues. He tried to press a dollar into Neecey's hands, but she let it drop to the floor.

"Take the money, you ungrateful girl," Ruby said as she tugged her crop top down. "He's being nice to you."

That coil of fear sprung and shot throughout her body when his sly fingers fondled her arm whenever he could under Ruby's neglectful eye.

"Girl, you doing all right," Della commented one Saturday as she pressed Neecey's hair. She sat in front of the stove.

Neecey, with a cloth diaper clenched between her teeth, sat on the floor between Della's knees. "And Keith ain't that bad-looking."

"I've had enough of yellow men to last a lifetime." Ruby laughed as she rocked two-year-old Serenda on her knees. Ruby sat between the breakfront and the kitchen table. She nursed a twelve-ounce bottle of Pepsi-Cola and nibbled on a bag of fat beer nuts. From the balcony, Jack and Odessa's playful voices drifted through the open kitchen window along with a cool breeze. The odor of Neecey's scorching hair filled the kitchen, in spite of the breeze. Neecey avoided the smell by sniffing the Jergen's Lotion on Della's legs.

"Yo' first husband, huh?" Della asked.

Neecey closed her eyes as Della maneuvered the sizzling hot comb through her nappy hair. She rolled her hands in the diaper and twisted tightly as the heat mingled with the grease and sweat on her scalp. She bit into the diaper to stifle her cries. Finally she heard the comb hit the eye of the stove and opened her eyes. She took deep breaths as Della's nimble fingers parted another section of hair. Extremely tender-headed (the barest touch of a comb on her scalp caused Neecey pain), Neecey was grateful to Della for pressing her hair. Della was easier on the head than Ruby, who yanked and pulled Neecey's hair like she was pulling yarn through a latch-hooked rug. Still, it was the diaper between her clenched teeth that kept her from screaming in pain.

"He was a good man," Ruby answered, "but laudy, why men wanna marry babies I'll never know."

"Why'd you think I left Georgia?" Della said. "My folks had plans for me to marry the oldest man in the county. I swear he was born before Emancipation."

Neecey watched Ruby's feet bump repeatedly against the

floor. Her legs rose and fell as her hand patted Serenda on the back. A continuous, reverberating *waaaaaaaah* rolled from Serenda's small mouth.

"Girl, naw! Let me tell you. Half the women in Copiah County wanted Mr. Milton," Ruby said. "My auntie sold my land and me to Mr. Milton. Yeah, sold me like I was livestock."

"Chile, I know what you mean." Della laughed as she positioned Neecey's head so that she could see only the back of the black breakfront and the thin line of dust between it and the floor. "I loved my daddy, and my mama, rest her soul, was a good woman, but I wasn't about to marry a seventy-year-old man. Last time I saw her, we laughed about it. She thought I was gonna marry old no-count Willie Ray. He was a pretty thang, that Willie Ray. Hold still, Neecey. I told her I didn't stand a chance with Willie Ray. He wanted to get next to my baby sis. That girl was twelve but hotter than cayenne pepper."

"Well," Ruby said, "I called my auntie after I had Neecey. She had a hissie-fit right over the phone. Told me I was stupid to throw a good man like Mr. Milton away, and what about my children? Well, when I did call to talk to the children, he said I didn't have no children there. Worst thing I ever did was send my auntie that picture of Neecey. I thought the man was over all that, but you know the stink he created."

"Well, you and yo' auntie on the right track now," Della said.

"Ooow!" Neecey screamed as the hot iron comb touched her ear.

"Oh, baby, I'm so sorry," Della apologized. She blew on the ear and the pain stopped for one second. "Hold still. I got just a little more to go."

"Naw, she ain't a woman to be trusted. She still don't know about Jesse."

"Girl, you didn't tell her he was in— "

"Hush up!" Ruby quickly said.

"Oops!" Della said.

Ruby had not told the children that Jesse was locked away in Joliet State Penitentiary. When they asked about him, she ignored their questions. How could she change the man who held their bikes steady, who repaired their roller skates, who helped them tear into Christmas presents, who chastised them with a heavy hand and loved them with a heavier heart into some face behind bars? How could she take their daddy, their hero, and distort him into a bad man? She could not.

"Hell, I don't know if dark men are any better." Ruby laughed.

"So, you don't mind if I do a little flirting with yo' boarder?" Della asked.

"If you don't mind me telling Pete, go ahead," Ruby said.

"Girl, you know I couldn't bat an eye at another man." Della laughed.

"Uh-uh," Ruby agreed. "You are too square, too square."

Keith came and went so quickly in their lives that at times Neecey wasn't sure if he had existed.

IT WAS THE NIGHT BEFORE CHRISTMAS, and Neecey and her siblings were all dressed in pj's. Excitement rippled from child to child as they watched Tennessee Ernie Ford with his special guest Jay North on television. The living room was all festive with lights and decorations. Jack on the floor and Odessa on the couch disagreed on who had been the best child that year.

"Santa gonna leave you one ugly doll," Jack teased. "'Cause he don't like crybabies."

"Ain't no crybaby," Odessa whined. "And Santa don't like no bad boys. He gonna leave you a lump of coal."

Neecey, in the armchair with Serenda on her lap, said nothing but looked at the Christmas tree glittering and shimmering with lights and ornaments. Underneath there were no presents, not even a small box.

"Mama, is Santa bring all our presents?" she asked Ruby.

Ruby, standing at the stove in her tattered robe, stirred the last milk into a cocoa and sugar mixture. She ignored Neecey's question and tossed the empty milk carton into the garbage can next to the sink. She placed four cups on a serving tray along with the last of the homemade tea cakes. As if she didn't have enough worries. As if it wasn't hard enough scraping up this little portion of their Christmas tradition. Now they wanted more. Toys and presents. Worrying her.

"Mama?" Neecey called again.

"I don't wanna talk about no Santa Claus!" Ruby snapped. "Be grateful for this cocoa and these tea cakes. Worrying about tomorrow ain't gonna help you today."

The children fell quiet and concentrated upon Ernie and his troupe, the Top Twenty, singing a medley of Christmas songs. By the time Ruby set the tray of tea cakes and cocoa on the cocktail table, the final spotlight was upon Ernie as he sang "Some Children See Him." The children's festive mood had returned, and once again visions of sugarplums danced through their heads.

Ruby lifted Serenda out of Neecey's arms and found a spot on the sofa, out of their circle of anticipation. She was anxious to send them to bed. To get them out of her hair, so she could watch *The Untouchables* in peace. But if she sent them to bed too early, they would rise at the crack of dawn. Rise and search for what would not be under that tree. More than once, Ruby was tempted to say, *There ain't no such thing as Santa Claus.* Instead, she held a bottle of lukewarm cocoa in Serenda's mouth and watched the credits roll on television.

"I'm staying up all night," Jack said. "Imma watch for Santa Claus."

"But we ain't got no chimney," Odessa said.

"Santa Claus'll land on the balcony," Jack said.

"Don't worry," Neecey said, "he'll find a way in."

A loud knock on the door interrupted their chatter. The children looked from the door to Ruby.

"Who is it?" Ruby called.

"Ho! Ho! Ho!" came a deep voice.

"It's us!" Della called.

"Auntie Della!" Neecey bound from her chair and opened the door.

Della, Louise, and Pete stumbled into the house loaded with bags and packages.

"Santa dropped your presents off at my house," Ma'Dear said to the children. "He said we could have a Christmas early."

Ma'Dear sat on the sofa with fifteen-month-old Serenda on her lap. Serenda crunched the soft fur of the large stuffed polar bear in her hand. On the floor, Odessa changed her baby doll diaper once more, while Jack flipped the switch of his Lionel train off and on. While the Christmas lights blinked off and on, and Nat King Cole sang "chestnuts roasting on an open fire" on the phonograph, Neecey ignored the wool coat lying in the only box that she had received. The coat was red with a velvet collar—a beautiful coat, but she could not enjoy it. Her thoughts were envious . . .

Jack over there with his shiny red train going round and round that little town. And look at ole Odessa and her Tiny Tears doll and tea set. Rocking that ole thing just so she can see her eyes open

and close like a real little baby. And Serenda chewing on that
fluffy bear. How come they all got toys and not me? No Chatty
Cathy Doll. No bike. Nothing. You know why. You know why.

Della and Pete picked up empty boxes and discarded wrap-
ping paper. Ruby took a sleeping Serenda from Louise's lap
and eased around Neecey and Odessa sitting before the
Christmas tree. She carefully stepped over Jack's train set and
carried Serenda out of the room. Neecey picked up the small
china teapot and a cup.

"Put that down," Odessa said. "That's mine."

"I just wanna play with it."

"No, you'll break it."

"Odessa, don't be selfish," Della said as she walked into the
kitchen. "Share with your sister."

"Ma'Dear said it's mine by myself."

"Louise!"

"Odessa need to learn to take care of her stuff," Louise
said.

"Mama said bad kids don't get shit for Christmas!" Odessa
innocently informed everyone.

"Odessa!" Della exclaimed. "Lord, Jesus. Ruby need to tan
your tail."

"That's what Mama said."

"Ain't nobody gonna whup the child for repeating what
Ruby told her," Louise said as she walked around the table.

"Well, Santa Claus didn't bring Neecey nothing, so she
musta been bad," Odessa reasoned.

Louise chuckled and headed out of the room. "I'll be ready
to go when I come out the bathroom," she said.

Neecey was too ashamed to move, ashamed that somehow
Santa knew about Booker. Neecey wanted to rise from the
floor, but she could not. She stared at the bubble lights on the

Christmas tree. The liquid danced and glistened in each bulb. If she could lose herself in those dancing colors, she could find her daddy and he would buy her a bike and a doll.

"Neeccy, sugar," Della called. "Hang up your coat."

"Neecey, you can play with my train," Jack said.

Neecey shook her head, picked her new coat up, and carried it to the walk-in closet. Pete rustled her head as she passed. She did not look at him but went inside the closet and searched for a hanger.

"Ma'Dear oughta be ashamed of herself," Neeccy heard Della whispering to Pete. "If I hadda know she wasn't buying toys for Neecey, I woulda got the child more than a coat and underwear."

"Ma'Dear did good, Della," Pete said. "She didn't have to buy nothing for any of them."

"But to leave a grandchild out . . ."

"But she ain't . . ."

"Peter James Shade! Don't you say it. That child don't know any other family but us. Don't you dare say it."

Inside the closet, Neecey hid her face in the coat. *There ain't no Santa Claus!* Neecey thought. *Ruby's a big fat liar. Ma'Dear's a big fat liar too. They all big fat liars.* She hung the coat up, and, with a set jaw, went back into the living room.

chapter 6

SOME YOUNG JACK

SOMEBODY TOLD RUBY that she was a fine hen—ripe, plump, with plenty of thigh meat. Somebody told Ruby that the fire in her hair matched the fire in her eyes, which he was sure matched the fire in her thighs. Somebody showered Ruby with compliments and caresses until she succumbed with parted arms and parted thighs. That somebody was twenty-three-year-old David Hamilton. A tall ink-black man with processed hair as slick as sealskin, he was a shadow that passed the children as he slithered in and out of their home, a trinket that Ruby found and kept to herself.

Some days, eleven-year-old Neecey, seven-year-old Jack, and five-year-old Odessa found the apartment darkened. The drapes and doors were fastened against all light. They found two-year-old Serenda with inappropriate playthings—shoe polish, bric-a-brac, and once a fork near an electric outlet. They found her curled on the sofa with her thumb in her mouth and a fat welt across her leg. Upon seeing Neecey, she leaped in her arms and burrowed her head in Neecey's neck. Always Ruby, clutching her robe, rushed from her room.

"Shh! David's sleeping," she whispered. "Y'all take off y'all things and sit down."

"I got homework," Neecey said.

"Do it later," Ruby said. "I need you to keep these kids quiet."

"I got to use the bathroom," Odessa said.

"Hurry up and get back here."

"Can I have some milk and cookies?" Jack asked.

"No! Sit y'all asses on the couch and watch TV!" Ruby hissed.

The children shucked their jackets off and sat. Ruby placed an extension cord strategically on the cocktail table so that, from plug to socket, each child was threatened by a section. Always, Ruby returned to the bedroom and the children huddled together on the sofa and watched *Garfield Goose*, *The Mickey Mouse Club*, or *The Susan Show*.

In that room, the furniture and children looked dusty, worn, and abandoned, as if the owners had moved away and forgotten their valuables. Only the breakfront, facing the cocktail table and sofa, boasted life with its collection of clowns. The clowns danced and leaped, grinned and frowned, and looked upon that room of forgotten things.

Enchanted by Clutch Cargo, Popeye, or Donald Duck, the children would forget Ruby and David until even the rumbling of the el outside their window, the blare of traffic six stories below, the playful voices of children outside, and the clacking of Garfield Goose's beak could not sheath the noisy springs of Ruby's bed nor David's ostentatious voice saying, *Oooh, mama, mama*. Ruby's keening broke through the closed door and the concrete walls like a siren, on and on until it made a wah-wah sound in Jack's head as he pumped his hands faster and faster against his ears. When the bedroom door finally opened, a heavy funkiness preceded David into the living room. Giggling, Ruby staggered after him in her chenille robe. The funkiness bit into the children's senses, and shame washed over them as their mother stood in the open doorway with her arms wrapped around David.

"When are you coming back?" Ruby whined every time, and every time wariness crossed David's face.

He kissed her forehead quickly, peeled her arms from around his neck, and moved from her clutching thighs. Her question hung in the air as he bolted across the balcony and vanished around the corner.

One afternoon Della, who watched the children while Ruby worked, stumbled onto this parting scene. Ruby's robe gaped open as she stood in the open doorway with her naked body pressed against David. Her robe shielded only her back from her children on the sofa. Ruby's red hair, matted to her head on one side, was covered with cotton ticks and feathers. Through the open doorway, Della saw the children sitting like stones on the sofa.

"Ruby!" Della exclaimed. "You're standing naked before the world."

Ruby laughed nervously and uncurled herself from David's body. She belted the robe over her nakedness. A tight look passed over David's face. He recognized the prim Sunday school haughtiness on Della's face. She was dressed like any other matron, flowery hat, white pristine gloves, pocketbook with matching sensible shoes, and of course the disapproving sneer underneath the granite eyes.

"Della, this is David," Ruby introduced.

"Uh-uh," Della said.

David said a cocky *Hello* and pulled Ruby to him. His tongue snaked around her lips, then dove into her welcoming mouth. Ruby gasped and grabbed his arms. Della looked past them to the children sitting on the couch.

"Excuse me," she snapped, "may I pass?"

"See you, baby." David chucked Ruby's chin. With a mocking grin on his face, David sauntered across the balcony and around the corner.

Ruby laughed and wiped David's saliva from her mouth with the back of her hand. She pulled her robe closer to her body and patted her matted sweaty hair. She did not feel like dealing with Della when she was still flushed from David's body. Della followed Ruby into the apartment. When the door closed, shameful afternoon darkness cloaked the apartment. Sprints of sunlight danced along the edges of drawn drapes. Della crinkled her nose. Fiery rankness filled the apartment. It made Della think of the brothels and juke joints of her hometown; made her think of illicit acts in the afternoon between her aunt and the town's good reverend; and finally, it made her think of her cheating husband.

"Put on some coffee while I get some clothes on," Ruby said and rushed down the hall and into her bedroom.

Della's eyes adjusted to the dimness of the room. She walked between the television set and the cocktail table. On the sofa, the children were mute like ghosts. Neecey held Serenda, who sucked her thumb and fingered her short braids, which stuck out like miniature wheat stacks. Odessa held a rubber doll and twisted its head back and forth. Jack glared at Della. Ruby had stretched an extension cord across the children's laps like a restraint. A large leather strap curled around the white porcelain bowl filled with porcelain flowers on the cocktail table.

"How y'all children doing?" Della asked as she looked down at them.

In unison, they gave a weak, "Okay."

Hard knots throbbed in Della's temples. Her tiny face drew into a tight snarl. If she had children, they would be light as air, floating on her love, not bunched up on the couch like refugees. She marched to the window, leaned across the armchair, and threw the drapes back. Daylight barged into the room. She opened the windows. The November stench from the stockyards fought against the funk in the apartment. She took a deep breath and thought, *At least it's cleaner than what's going on in here.* When she turned, the children were blinking from the brightness.

"I'm sure my precious pumpkins are doing better than okay," she said.

The children stared blankly at her. Jack hunched his shoulders. Odessa poked a finger into the doll's empty eye socket. *Damn you, Ruby!* Della thought. She leaned over the table and snatched the extension cord from across the children's legs. They all flinched. Odessa drew up in a tight ball. Della tossed the extension cord toward the window. It landed on the chair. The children stared at the extension cord and, with an audible breath, relaxed. The stiffness of the afternoon melted from their bodies. Della moved toward the kitchen. She placed her pocketbook on the breakfront that divided the two rooms and removed her gloves and hat.

"Auntie?" Jack asked in a tiny voice that did not belong to him. "You got any Nut Chews?"

"Boy," Della gave a dry, hard laugh, thankful for the normalcy of his question. "You and yo' sweet tooth! Y'all had supper yet?"

"No ma'am," Neecey said.

"Odessa, wash yo' hands and come help me in the kitchen. Jack, you can have a Nut Chew after you eat. I swear this is sinful. Pure sinful," Della said and headed for the kitchen. Her face was tight with displeasure and her temples pulsated with anger.

Soon, the aroma of brewing coffee became a balm in the apartment. The apartment filled with the chatter and laughter of the children. They sat at the table, kicking their legs back and forth while they wolfed down pork and beans and hot dogs. The hard knots in Della's temples eased. She leaned against the counter with a cup of coffee and waited for Ruby.

"Girl, ain't he pretty?" Ruby asked and squeezed past Della and the table of children. The funk still surrounded her. She had not bathed or washed up. Instead, she had quickly slipped on a pair of capri pants and a blouse. Although her hair was still matted, the cotton ticks and feathers were gone. Della looked beyond Ruby's forced bravado to the nervous twitch in her jaw, the shaking of her hand as she lifted the percolator from the counter, the loudness of her voice.

"Maybe he's too damn pretty, Ruby," Della said. "He can't be no more than, what? Twenty-six?"

"He's twenty-three," Ruby said.

Coffee spurted from Della's mouth onto her white blouse. "Great Scott, Ruby. You're thirty-five!" Della shouted.

Della set the cup on the counter and grabbed the dish towel. Ruby didn't look around. She carried her coffee into the living room and walked straight to the window. The drapes fluttered in the breeze through the window and brushed against Ruby's hand. She set her coffee cup on the windowsill and pushed the drapes further back. Raymond Elementary School loomed on the other side of the el tracks. Red, orange, and gold autumn leaves decorated the school's visible windows. The leaves resembled confetti thrown against the glass. David filled Ruby's soul with confetti, with a party of laughter and music. Ruby wanted to hold on to that feeling. She would not let sourpuss Della take this from her. She walked to the sofa and curled in a corner.

Ruby watched Della rinse most of the coffee stain from her blouse with cold water. Della poured more coffee into a cup but wanted something stronger than coffee. She needed a Pepsi.

"Y'all, don't touch those cookies until all that food is gone," Della said to the children.

"Can we go outside after we eat?" Jack turned in his chair and looked up at her.

"Yeah," she answered and rubbed the top of his head.

She dug into her pocket, pulled out her cigarettes, and lit one on the stove. The tip turned first yellow, then red, and Della realized that Ruby was changing into the type of woman they had disparagingly gossiped about. The type of woman who snubbed common decency for a few tantalizing crumbs of pleasure. Della took a long drag from the cigarette. Puffs of smoke followed her from the kitchen to the armchair.

"Why are you here so early?" Ruby asked.

Every evening, Pete dropped off Della and picked up Ruby for work. Every morning Della, Jack, Neecey, and Odessa rushed out the door as Ruby entered, barely staying awake to take care of Serenda. The arrangement worked out well, since Pete also worked the night shift at Primo Cookie Company.

"Pete had to go in early," Della said. She balanced the cup and saucer on the arm of the chair. "You gotta take the bus tonight. Do that boy know how old you are?"

Ruby stretched her arms across the back of the sofa. The movement reminded Della of a sated cat. She waited for Ruby's answer. The wind stirred the drapes behind her. Another whiff from the stockyards flew past Della's head. Dark shadows fell across the coffee table. Della waited, but Ruby flicked imaginary dirt from beneath her fingertips and said nothing.

"Do he know how old you are?" Della repeated.

"I told him I was twenty-six."

"Twenty-six!" Della's tiny eyes widened. "How old do he think Neecey is?"

"I told him I had to get married when I was fifteen," Ruby said. She looked at her fingernail and thought, *Go away.*

"Laud, Ruby!"

"That's true enough."

"Don't go falling in love with this boy, Ruby."

"Why not?" Ruby turned and looked at Della. "He's crazy about me."

"You be careful, girl," Della warned. "These young boys look for older women to take care of them."

"You don't even know him," Ruby said.

"First thing they do," Della spoke absently, "is ask for a small loan."

"Della, don't get all knotted up."

"First they ask for twenty dollars and then fifty dollars, and Ruby, you'll never get anything back but a hump."

"You're being mean," Ruby said.

"I'm being real, Ruby."

"I've lent him money and he's paid me back."

"You're lending him money?"

"He paid me back."

"You barely make enough to take care of these children!" Della cried. "Look around, Ruby! This is the best shape you've been in since Jesse got sent away! Don't mess this up with some young jack!"

"He's crazy about me, Della," Ruby said.

"Don't put yo' all in this thang. You'll be in a worse fix than before."

"You always make a mess where there ain't no trash," Ruby said. She rose, stretched, and walked toward the hall.

"Ruby!" Della called. Ruby stopped but did not turn around. "I've known you to do some crazy things, but ain't never known you to play a fool."

From the balls of her feet, to the crown of her head, Ruby straightened her body, walked down the hall, and into her bedroom. Della knocked the ashes off her cigarette and took a final drag.

SOME DAYS the children arrived home from school and knew that David had come and gone. Ruby would radiate, pulsing like the sun on a hazy day. On those days, she was generous and playful, a hen brooding over her flock. Laughter rang throughout the apartment. She fussed over them, smooched faces, tossed Serenda up in the air, danced to Fats Domino's "Hail Hail Rock and Roll," and told outrageous stories of farm life.

I useta slop the pigs with my cousins. We would climb up on the railings of the sty and throw the food over and watch those little oinkers come running. Just throw the food on the ground. Useta love to see them eating with their snouts all nasty with dirt. Let me tell you, they had so much hair in their ears and nose that little bugs would make their home in it. One day my cousin fell in and I swear the pigs started nibbling on her. That girl was crawling around that pig sty, getting all muddy and stanky, and we were laughing. 'Cause Dora was a biggie. She was screaming, "Help me! Help me!" Big as a hog and screaming for somebody to save her.

Finally, the children encircled her, singing: *Ring around mama, a pocketful of mama, ashes, ashes, we all fall down.*

The children would make her stumble onto the couch and tickle her silly until she yelled, "Uncle, Uncle!" Too soon, it would be bedtime. Monday through Friday, Della would climb out of Uncle Pete's car and Ruby would replace her. Ruby and Pete made their way to the bakery, where they would work until morning making vanilla wafers and crackers. Morning would come and Ruby would stumble into the apartment. Della would stumble out of the apartment and join Pete for the drive to their new home. And the children would go merrily to school only to come home to a darkened apartment and *Shh! David is sleeping.*

Ruby plunged deeper into her affair with David. Like a magus, she presented David with her most precious gifts: her body, her food, and her money. She courted David with steak and eggs while the children survived on lima beans and a hunk of corn bread. Ruby wooed David with packages from Robert Hall or Bond's Department Store while her children wore thrift-store clothes. She seduced David with Florsheim's shoes while her children's feet ached in their Ben's two-pairs-for-five-dollars shoes.

David rewarded her with a continually singing bed. Yet these concerts only invoked a deeper hunger within Ruby. When days passed with no visit or word from David, she became malicious toward her children. "If it wasn't for y'all snot-nosed kids, David would move in," she yelled and the extension cord would crackle against their backs and legs at the slightest provocation: a movement too slow, a wrong word, or a misunderstood look.

"I hate him," Jack whispered to Neecey. "I wanna kill him."

"Me too," Odessa whispered.

"We all want him to disappear," Neecey agreed.

Two-year-old Serenda knew only that the extension cord around her mother's neck meant don't move, don't cry, and don't breathe.

chapter 7

THE BEAT

O NE SATURDAY, the air ricocheted with voices of children now freed from their winter's hibernation. They yelled, shrieked, and screamed with abandonment. Neecey, standing on the balcony, gently kneaded a water balloon. She rubbed one foot against a leg. Welts and sores covered her legs. The three thick braids on her head were matted and caked with dirt and grease. Her socks slipped into her shoes. Odessa stooped in the corner between the kitchen window and the cinder-block wall that separated the balcony from the passageway. She pulled her dress as far down as she could. Her teeth chattered and goose bumps puckered along her arms and legs. Jack stood next to Neecey at the fence. Jack's caramel eyes sparkled mischievously as he eyed the balloon in Neecey's hand.

"Throw it, Neecey," he urged.

Neecey played recklessly with the water balloon. She eyed the tall chain-link fence that ran the length of the balcony from their apartment to the Thomas's apartment. If she threw the balloon out far enough, it would land on the sidewalk below. If not, it would probably land on a balcony on its way down. Neecey looked below. The men outside Stateway Liquor Store passed a bag among themselves. Their boisterous voices filled the air with cusses and laughter. A few people were walking on the sidewalk in front of the building. She could see the tops of their heads.

"Do it, Neecey," Odessa urged. She tugged one thick wavy braid against her face.

Sweat popped across Neecey's nose. Her eyes burned. Everyone would see her. Ruby would beat the skin off her body. Ruby would kill her. Down the passageway, the doors leading to the bank of elevators opened. Neecey heard footsteps.

"Do it now!" Jack urged her.

Neecey didn't move. The image of Ruby beating the skin off her body was grounded in her soul. Jack snatched the balloon. He backed up to the kitchen window, ran up to the fence, and threw the balloon. It wobbled over the fence. Jack and Neecey jumped back from the fence to the kitchen window. Yells came from the ground.

"Damn!" David laughed as he turned the corner. "Y'all some bad little crumb snatchers. Yo' mama home?"

"Yeah," Neecey said.

Maybe the wind carried his voice to Ruby's ears, or maybe it was some base instinct that propelled her. Ruby burst through the door like an attacking dog and leaped into David's arms. David staggered back and bumped into Jack. Ruby held onto him and curled around him like a boa constrictor. She kissed his face, his neck, and his lips. Her body strained through the thin fabric of her housedress. Odessa rose from the corner and stepped over to Neecey. Jack turned his back to the couple, balled his hands into fists, and stuck them in his pockets. An el rumbled over the tracks that ran behind the liquor store. The children scuffled their feet and fidgeted. Odessa shivered and Neecey put her arm around her shoulder.

"Where have you been?" Ruby asked.

Don't ask him that, Neecey thought.

"Hey!" He laughed and pulled her arms away. "I've been busy, babe."

"Come in," she tugged at him.

"Mama, can we come in?" Jack asked.

Ruby released her hold on David and half turned to the children. She glared at them. Her swollen eyes were as red as her hair.

"It's cold," Neecey said.

"Y'all wanted to play outside," Ruby snapped.

"It's getting dark," Neecey said.

"You're not coming in here with a bunch of racket."

"We're cold and hungry, Ruby," Neecey said.

Jack and Odessa looked at Neecey. Her hazel eyes held baleful defiance. Her face was tight, free of fear. Her voice sounded much like the spewing of a nasty lump of mucus from the back of the throat. Ruby and Neecey stood close together on that tiny balcony, with only David's arm between them. David squeezed between Ruby and the fence and walked to the door. Jack and Odessa looked at Neecey with wide eyes. They waited for Ruby to slap, kick, or sling Neecey around. They waited for Ruby to reclaim her authority. She did not. Instead, Ruby trailed behind David into the apartment. Neecey rushed to the door and grabbed it before it slammed in their faces.

"Neecey, wash yo' hands and make some sandwiches," Ruby ordered.

Jack and Odessa skirted around Ruby and headed for their room. Neecey stomped out of the room. *Why can't you cook your own children some food?* she thought. *I betcha if he wanted to eat, you get up and make a big meal. I betcha even make him* *a cake. Don't like him anyway. All over him like that.*

"I can't stay," David said.

See, Neecey thought. *He doesn't even like you.*

"Ain't seen you in days," Ruby said.

The children rushed down the hallway into their room. Odessa curled in a tight ball on the bed that she shared with Neecey. Her teeth chattered loudly.

"Oh, man!" Jack exclaimed when he saw Serenda sprawled in his bed. "How come she's always in my bed? She gets my bed all wet. How come she's not in her baby bed?"

"Don't wake her!" Neecey warned.

"I'm so cold," Odessa said. Her teeth chattered loudly.

"Jack, throw a blanket over her," Neeccy said as she tossed her jacket onto the pile of clothes peeking out of the closet.

"She can get her own blanket," he retorted.

"Do you want to eat?" Neecey threatened. She and Jack passed mean, malevolent looks at each other. Neecey folded her arms across her chest, raised one eyebrow, and silently commanded him to *do it!*

"Man!" he exclaimed and dragged a blanket off his bed and threw it across Odessa and Serenda. "Sick of girls. Sick! Sick! Sick!" He punched his pillow with each word.

"Y'all stay here until I fix something to eat," Neecey said. She removed her jacket and tossed it on Jack's bed.

"Make me a peanut butter sandwich," Jack said. He dragged his hands along the porous cinder-block walls—over the purple crayon marks made by Serenda, over the red marks made by Odessa, and over the blue cars he had drawn.

"Imma cook," Neecey said.

"You can't cook," Jack said.

"I'm going to cook today," Neecey said. "I don't want peanut butter. Stay here and keep out of Ruby's way."

After washing her hands, Neecey hurried past the kissing couple on the couch. Ruby moved over David like a cat starved for affection. She curled on his lap and stroked his face and chest. She smothered him with kisses while emitting tiny moans from her throat.

Alone in the kitchen, Neecey opened the refrigerator and eyed the bologna in its yellow and red package. She could fry the bologna and slap it between slices of bread with mayonnaise or she could take that hunk of ground beef sitting next to it and make juicy burgers with tomatoes. The thought of crisp sweet relish on her tongue made up Neecey's mind. She opened a bottom cabinet and banged her knee. She set a cast iron skillet on the stove and accidentally smashed her finger. The pain in her finger and knee could not smother her awareness of Ruby begging David like a wino begging for a drink.

"Come to my room for a minute," Ruby pleaded.

"I told you I got somebody waiting," he said.

"Please."

"I'll come by Tuesday," David said.

Don't! Neecey thought. She placed four hamburger-sized patties in the skillet.

"I'm trying to take care of some business, mama," he said. "I just come by to ask for a favor."

"What kinda favor?"

"I need a hundred dollars."

Money, Neecey thought. *Just like Aunt Della said. He just wants your money.*

"I don't have a hundred dollars," Ruby said. "I just have five dollars for the kids' lunches for the next month."

Don't give him my lunch money, Ruby, Neecey thought. She

removed the Blue Diamond matchbox from the drawer and struck one. She turned on the gas. Gas and fire swooshed and burned the tip of her fingers. She dropped the match down the eye of the stove.

"That's all?" David asked incredulously. "I thought you got paid yesterday."

"I did," Ruby whined, "but I had to pay rent and buy some groceries."

Yeah, hamburger and pork and beans for her children, Neecey thought. She pulled a chair against the sink.

"So what I'm supposed to do?" David asked. "I thought I could depend on you."

You can depend on her more than we can, Neecey thought, and removed a can of pork and beans from the cabinet over the sink.

"You can." Ruby clung to him.

See, told you, Neecey thought.

"Damn, baby," he said. "You can't help me at all?"

Nope! Neecey thought. She ain't got any money for you. She found the can opener in the drawer and realized she didn't know how to use it. She tried to stick the sharp point into the can. It skidded across the top and knocked the can over.

"Please, come to the bedroom for a minute."

Don't beg, Ruby, Neecey thought. She banged the sharp point into the can. She nicked one finger in the process of half opening the can. The hamburgers sizzled, releasing a continuous hiss of steam. Neecey turned the fire down as she had seen Ruby do many times. She opened the refrigerator. She examined the shelves and tallied the food that was never enough. She removed two tomatoes from a bowl and slammed the refrigerator.

"I told you, my time is short," he said. "I'm trying to raise money for a business deal. Can't you borrow the money from that snotty sister-in-law of yours?"

Neecey silently snorted to herself. *Aunt Della! Never.*

"Please come back to the room for just one minute," Ruby implored. "I need to talk to you."

Go home, Neecey thought.

"Ruby, I don't have time for that."

"I'm having a baby!" Ruby blurted.

A baby! Neecey looked around at the red and white gingham curtains, at the Formica table and tufted-back chairs, at the plaster fruit plaques on the wall next to the refrigerator, at the cat clock with its tail and eyes moving in time to its tick tock. Oh, no. She had not stepped into Narnia. No, no. She had not fallen down the rabbit hole. No, no, no! She was not somewhere over the rainbow. She was home, home where the babies roam.

Neecey pierced the hamburger patties with a fork as she had seen Ruby do a thousand times. Blood ran from the center. Neecey turned the hamburgers. Like an incessant nudge, the quiet from the living room bothered Neecey. She looked past the breakfront. Ruby sat on David's lap and picked at the zipper on his jacket. Hardness washed over David's face as he stared out the window.

"How soon can we get married?" Ruby asked.

"Married?" David laughed.

He crudely pushed Ruby off his lap and onto the sofa. A solid thud resounded as his legs knocked against the table in his haste to extricate himself.

"David, I'm pregnant," she said.

"Why're you telling me?" he looked down at her. "You ain't saddling me with a bunch of bad little crumb snatchers."

"What?" Ruby asked in a small, weak voice. Ruby's mouth dropped as she looked at him. Ruby shook her head. She did not understand his words nor his meanness.

"Hey, I'm only up here in the afternoons," he said. His eyes were small pockets of darkness. "And not that often. Do you see my point?"

"No," Ruby whispered.

"I mean, damn, baby, whatcha do with yo' nights?" He shrugged.

"What?" she asked again.

"Oh, come on, Ruby. The gig is up." David threw up his hands. "We had our fun, but I'm not taking the rap for some other man's baby."

"I don't sleep around," she said.

"You slept with me," he said.

"I love you," she said.

"Look, mama, you're too old for this weepy stuff." A nasty laugh followed that statement. Neecey thought of villainous Dastardly Dan from the Dudley Do-Right cartoons.

"But you said you love me," Ruby cried.

"I hope you know how to take care of these things," David said, "'cause I'm not playing daddy to no brat."

He squeezed between the table and Ruby on the sofa. Ruby grabbed his shirt. David stumbled in his haste to escape her clutches. He jerked away from her grasp. Ruby slipped to the floor and grabbed his leg.

"I love you," Ruby declared, clinging to his leg. "Please, don't leave me."

Neecey, holding the rinsed tomatoes in a dish towel, watched in horror as David walked toward the door, dragging Ruby with him. He grabbed Ruby by her short red hair and shoved her off his leg. Ruby squealed like a dying pig and lay crumpled against the table as he rushed out the door. David bolted across the balcony and around the corner.

"David!" Ruby screamed.

Neecey grimaced and shook her head. She walked to the end of the table and stood with her back to the wall. Using a butcher knife, Neecey began to cut one of the tomatoes. *Whatcha crying for,* Neecey thought. *He only wanted your money.*

"David!" Ruby's cries penetrated the pores of the cinder-block wall until each pore filled with sorrow, until that sorrow crescendoed into a wail that brought the younger children from the back bedroom. Serenda, crying, toddled down the hall behind Jack and Odessa. The sight of those glassy-eyed children propelled Ruby into rage.

"You little shits!" she yelled. She rose from the floor. "I'll teach you to throw water balloons. Pissy ass kids, running a good man away."

Ruby stormed through the apartment. The frightened children milled around like lost souls. Tears and snot ran down all their faces. In the living room Odessa, ever nervous, clutched the hem of her dress. Jack danced from one foot to the next. Serenda rubbed her fist against her cheek. Their wails joined Ruby's wails in the pores of the walls.

"I didn't do nothing," Jack cried.

"Oh, Lordy, Lordy," Odessa cried.

"I'm sorry, Mama," Serenda cried.

"Bad-ass little kids," Ruby shouted as she searched her room and their room for the extension cord. The apartment rocked with rage, sorrow, and fear. Serenda ran into the kitchen and hid behind Neecey. Neecey moved closer to the table and sliced the tomato into huge slices.

Ruby flew out of the children's bedroom into the hall

closet. Soon Ruby, with extension cord in hand, emerged from the closet and charged up the hall. The extension cord swished across Odessa's back. Her thin blouse burst open from the force. Odessa screamed and danced as the hot pain coursed through her body. Jack, who was trapped in the living room, began a song of mercy.

"Please, don't whup me, Mama. Please, don't whup me."

The extension cord rose above the breakfront and descended once again. Odessa fell to the floor in screams. Welts and blood burst from her skin. Rage distorted Ruby's face.

"You act like wild heathens!" Ruby hissed through her closed teeth. She swirled around and caught Jack across the back. He screamed and managed to run past Ruby before she could weld another lick. Odessa, afraid that Ruby would again focus on her, crawled to the end of the sofa, then squeezed into the corner between the window and the end table. Ruby, however, had redirected her anger toward Jack. She followed him into the kitchen, where he cowered in the corner with Serenda.

"Please, Mama!" he cried.

Serenda's cries merged with that plea. Only Neecey seemed unaffected by the rage. She stood at the table, whacking away at the second tomato. Ruby whiffed the air like a bloodhound.

"Who gave you permission to cook hamburgers?" Ruby screamed. The extension cord cut across Neecey's back and caught Jack in the face. He screamed and grabbed his face. The tight corner held a mass of activities. Serenda crawled under the table and out the other side. Jack followed her. He dodged Ruby and ran into the living room. Cornered by the cinder-block wall, and unable to pass Ruby, Neecey pivoted back and forth.

"You told me to fix something," Neecey screamed. "You told me to fix something."

"Heifer! Cooking my food!" Ruby yelled. She wielded the extension cord like a whip. Neecey moved back against the table. The extension cord bit into her arm. Neecey screamed as the pain traveled up that arm. She staggered against the table.

"No," Neecey shouted. She grabbed the knife from the table and held it in front of herself. Ruby saw the knife and took a step back.

"I'll kill you if you hit me again," Neecey said. "I'll kill you."

"Kill me!" Ruby screamed. "You'll kill me?"

Ruby flicked the extension cord and it whipped around Neecey's arm. Neecey screamed and dropped the knife. Ruby grabbed Neecey by her top braid and pulled the child to her chest. Spinning around, she flung Neecey toward the living room. Neecey stumbled and fell against the breakfront. The breakfront toppled over and all the clowns shattered as they hit the hard concrete floor. The children, screaming, scrambled out of the way.

"Kill me!" Ruby shouted and flicked the cord against the girl's back.

Neecey arched her back from the lick and screamed, "Jesus! Jesus!"

In an attempt to escape the lashes, Neecey tripped over the breakfront and fell to the floor. Bits of broken glass cut into her knees and arms.

"Neecey!" the children screamed.

The sound of her name from their lips soaked into her heart. Neecey tried to crawl away from the lashes upon her back. Her hands and knees fell upon more glass, but Neecey was beyond cries and screams. Terror had made her mute. She looked toward Jack and Serenda. They stood in openmouthed terror in the hallway. Odessa whimpered from her corner. Neecey held on to those sounds and the odor of burning hamburger. She had to hold on to those things or she would die. She would die.

Ruby screamed and grabbed Neecey's hair. She pulled Neecey out the broken porcelain and ceramic, only to fling her toward the couch. Neecey's head bounced against the back of the couch and Ruby pounced on her. She slapped Neecey's face back and forth, back and forth, until Neecey slumped into unconsciousness.

chapter 8

BABY BLUES

SPRING AND SUMMER had come and gone since Ruby announced another child was on the way. It was a difficult pregnancy. Her movement slowed to a sloth-like wobble. Her bed became her nest, her sanctuary. David, true to his word, had disappeared, and although she still lived in the apartment, Ruby had disappeared too. Her mourning was an endless thing. She broke into tears while watching television, sipping coffee, or sleeping. She wailed and lamented, *David, David, David.* She functioned with the least amount of effort to get through the next minute, the next hour, the next day.

"Girl, you gotta snap out of this," Della said. "You got children to think about."

The children cringed at the mention of their existence. How well they remembered Ruby's rage when she beat Neecey into unconsciousness. *Please, please,* they collectively and silently begged. *Don't mention us. Let us be.* The children were content to be invisible before Ruby. They learned to exist, to survive in spite of her.

Della saw the welts and bruises on Neecey's arms and legs and asked, "What this child do, Ruby? What she do?"

"Just knocked over my breakfront," Ruby lied. "Broke up all my stuff."

"Mercy!" Della declared. "Look at her arms!"

"She ain't dead," Ruby answered. "We all done got our fair share of whuppings and then some."

Della shut her mouth because she had received her share of whuppings. Still the welts itched at her. They appeared randomly on Jack, on Odessa, but most of all Neecey. The children were close mouthed when she asked, "Whacha do, child? Whacha do?"

"Listen, you got a problem with the way I raise my children, take them home with you!" Ruby snapped.

While her heart ached, they *were* Ruby's children. Pete reminded her of that often enough. It was Ruby who struggled to feed and clothe them, and that became difficult after her job forced her onto maternity leave. Still, Ruby managed with the few dollars that Louise and Pete begrudgingly contributed for the children and the money sent by her aunt in Mississippi.

The children found it easier to put their wants and needs before twelve-year-old Neecey. They had only to look at the snakelike scar on Neecey's arm to remember Ruby's rage. They had only to make one tiny mistake for the extension cord to appear. So they ignored the big woman with the mean gray eyes and went straight to Neecey. "Neecey, can we have a peanut butter and jelly sandwich? Neecey, I need some clean clothes for school. Neecey, I bumped my head. Neecey, I'm cold." Neecey this. Neecey that. Neecey. Neecey. Neecey.

Neecey's name became a liturgy that she hated, and Ruby was some hard-fisted woman cracking the broom against her back, throwing kitchen chairs at her, cussing and screaming, *You're a lazy ass cow. All you wanna do is eat and sleep.* Didn't matter that she had to wash the dishes, clean the bathroom, mop floors, and bring ice water to Ruby, who spent a lot of time crying and sleeping. Didn't matter that Serenda was now her child to change and bathe and to discipline with no-no. The wrong move, the wrong word, the wrong look, and Ruby would snatch her by her braids and twirl her around or toss a pot at her like it was a blown kiss.

THE SMELL OF BURNT RICE FILLED THE KITCHEN, yet the children sat around the table and eagerly waited for Neecey to spoon watery gravy over her portion. The sticky clumps of rice sported a dark undercoat. She carried her plate to the table and eased into her chair.

"Can we eat now?" asked eight-year-old Jack.

"Bow your heads," Neecey said to the children. The children dropped their heads, and Neecey whispered, "We thank you for this food, Jesus."

"Amen," Jack said and immediately attacked the food.

The scraping forks and spoon created a rhythm as the children ate. Three-year-old Serenda used her hand to pick up the tough slice of liver. She bit into it and pulled to tear off a portion. Jack, sitting before the space where the breakfront once stood, shoveled the rice and gravy into his mouth, chewed a couple of times, and swallowed.

"This is good, Neecey," he said.

Only Odessa, sitting before the window, was displeased with the meal. She stabbed her fork into the liver again and again. She pushed the hard peas around her plate, and barely nibbled at the rice and gravy.

"What is this? It feels like a rubber ball," she said.

"Liver," Neecey said.

"This ain't liver," Odessa said. "Ruby's liver is soft."

Mama had disappeared from the children's vocabulary. Mama had no place in their tiny apartment of fear and hunger. Mama made apple turnovers and kept a spic-and-span house. Mama sang and rocked her children to sleep. Ruby was not a *Mama*. She never acknowledged the children's switch from *Mama* to Ruby. She was too young, she said to the air that flitted in and out her door, to be saddled with so many ungrateful children. Ruby cried and fussed and cussed and wished that all those children hanging around her skirt tails would drop away.

"When I grow up, ain't never eating liver," Odessa said. She stabbed at the liver until it was filled with perforations.

"When I grow up, Imma eat chicken and french fries every day," Jack said.

"Apple pie," Neecey said and slipped into her chair. "Imma have apple pie every day."

"More," Serenda said and pushed her plate across the table to Neecey. "Gimme some more."

"And Imma have somebody cook for me," she said as she rose from the table. "And ain't gonna have no children."

Years later, when nieces and nephews traipsed through her home, she would not remember that statement, but would touch her empty womb and wonder why she never made time to marry and have babies.

THE FIRST DAY OF SIXTH GRADE, twelve-year-old Neecey fell in love with tall, boney Miss Cole. Miss Cole's dark eyes crinkled and sparkled. She filled the classroom with music from large black and pink musical notes that bordered the ceiling to miniature musical instruments scattered around the room. A white upright piano stood in the far corner of the room. Even the science table exhibited a set of bells, along with a colorful aquarium.

Miss Cole's class was a universe away from Neecey's home. Quickly, she leaped over fractions, colonial history, and the makeup of a simple leaf. She became the teacher's helper and the teacher's pet. If only she could stay in that room, stay under the watchful eye of Miss Cole, no one would hurt her.

The most humiliating moment of her life happened in Miss Cole's room. Miss Cole celebrated every holiday and the birthdays of all her favorite musicians from Chopin to Coltrane by plopping an LP on her small record player and passing out cookies and juice to the students. In January, the class celebrated Wolfgang Amadeus Mozart's birthday by munching on cookies shaped like quarter notes and apple juice. Neecey, who had eaten only toast the night before and no breakfast or lunch, promptly threw up the sweets. While the school janitor cleaned Neecey's desk, Miss Cole helped her clean herself in the girl's washroom.

"Pamela," Miss Cole asked as she washed the front of Neecey's plaid dress, "do you have food at home?"

Neecey, humiliated by the vomit, looked down from Miss Cole's wide round eyes. Shame flushed across her back, her neck, into her face. She wanted the black and white tile beneath her feet to open up and swallow her. If she could bury her head like a tortoise, if she could roll up like a sow bug, if she could hide until school was out.

"Where's the shame in not having food?" Miss Cole asked as she wiped Neecey's hand. Neecey noticed a smaller, sixth finger growing out of Miss Cole's little finger. If she looked at the finger long enough, maybe it would be magical and make all the shame disappear. The little finger remained still, and the day continued in its miserable way. Tears of shame scalded her cheeks.

"Pamela, if you have problems at home, you can talk to me."

"Yes, ma'am," Neecey said.

How could she tell Miss Cole about forcing bread down or eating spaghetti with oleo or how Booker Strickland messed with her? Miss Cole lifted her chin and wiped her eyes.

"You can tell me anything," she whispered, "anything."

Neecey took the weekend to think. She wrote the note in her best handwriting. *Maybe,* she thought, *when Miss Cole read this note, she'll take me home with her. And all the men in the world will turn into lightning bugs. And I'll snatch them from the air. I'll pluck their lights out, then squash them.* That Monday, Neecey slipped the note under Miss Cole's attendance book.

In her fifteenth year of teaching Lorraine Cole would win the American Association of Educators' Teacher of the Year award. Between the moment she found Pamela Shade's note and the moment she clasped the golden apple, Lorraine crusaded for more in-depth counseling for students within the public school system. She always believed that showing the note to Pamela's mother was the most tragic error of her teaching career.

Although Lorraine had specifically asked to meet with Pamela's mother before class and alone, the girl's mother came while class was in session. When the door opened and the huge woman wobbled into the classroom with Pamela at her side, every movement, every sound in the room ceased. Lorraine tried to keep her eyes from the woman's stomach. Yet she was short, round, and shaped like a hot-air balloon with arms and legs. Instinctively, Lorraine knew that funny pictures of the woman would circulate around her classroom. She took the note from her top drawer and quickly walked to the huge woman and Pamela.

"Mrs. Shade, it would be better if we discussed this in the hall, alone," she said.

"I want Neecey right there," Ruby said and dragged Neecey into the hall with them.

"Class, I want it quiet and finish the problems on page ninety," Lorraine said as walked toward the door.

Lorraine closed the classroom door behind her and waited until the fourth-grade teacher passed them and entered his classroom. The long drafty corridor shrunk into a hot box in which they crowded together. Neecey scuffed one shoe upon the other. When Lorraine looked into the woman's face, she met a pair of steely gray eyes. Lorraine saw no concern, no warmth, only a bristling cold anger.

"If you got a problem with her, tell me," Ruby snapped and folded her arms across her chest.

"Pamela wrote this in class," Miss Cole said, and handed the note to Ruby.

In her best handwriting Neecey had written: *All the men in the world follow me. They touch me. They feel me and do it to me.* Lorraine, who was focusing on Ruby's expression, did not see the tears running down Neecey's face nor the furtive glances Neecey made toward Ruby's coat pocket and the glint of a belt buckle. When the note fluttered from Ruby's hand, Lorraine thought the woman had gone into shock. Neecey, however, saw Ruby's hand snatch the belt from her pocket and immediately clung to Miss Cole.

"No, Ruby!" she cried.

Ruby snatched Neecey from the teacher and flipped the belt against her legs, covered only by wool knee-high socks. Shocked, Miss Cole watched the woman lash the child.

"Nasty! Nasty! Nasty!" Ruby shouted repeatedly, and with each *nasty* she whipped the belt against the child's legs.

Neecey's howls filled the hallway. The scuttling sound of chairs and desks came from the classroom. In her pain, Neecey heard the rush of a thousand feet, the opening of doors, and voices from classrooms. She saw the stunned faces and Miss Cole standing with her mouth open. Somebody shouted, *She's getting a whupping at school.*

"Mrs. Shade, don't . . ." Lorraine grabbed Ruby's hand. Ruby tried to pull away, but Lorraine held her.

"Lorraine, do you need help?" another teacher asked.

"It's okay. I got it," Lorraine said.

Neecey hid behind Lorraine and clung to her. Her tears and mucus soaked and stained Lorraine's blue rayon dress. Lorraine felt the thin fingers digging into her side. She dropped Ruby's hand and held Neecey against her side. Neecey sobbed. Tremors ran through her body.

"There's a problem," Lorraine said, trying to suppress the anger that was rising against the woman. Hunger, terror. What else was going on in the child's life? "I think Pamela is asking for help."

"Twelve years old and turning into a slut!" Ruby yelled. "I'm sending you to school for an education and you're writing dirty notes."

"Maybe we can talk after you calm down," Lorraine said.

"What's to talk about?" Ruby said. "She's been messing around with boys and sitting up in class writing about it. All I go through for y'all and you act like this!"

All the words Lorraine intended to say, all the comfort and reassurance, all her two semesters of psychology and good intentions disappeared. She had intended to talk reasonably and sympathetically with Mrs. Shade.

"Pamela, is there something you want to tell us about the note?" Lorraine asked.

Neecey shook her head. What was there to say? If she could be invisible like air and drift away from the school, from Ruby, from her life. If only.

"Fast tail!" Ruby snapped. "You better not write another dirty note or have another dirty thing come out your mouth."

"Maybe you need time to think about this, Mrs. Shade," Lorraine said while holding on to Neecey. "When you calm down, maybe you and Pamela could talk about this."

"Ain't nothing more to say," Ruby said. "I'll take her home . . ."

"No," Lorraine said as Neecey fingers dug into her. "Let her finish the school day."

Ruby looked from the woman to her daughter and shrugged. She swirled around and left the teacher and girl standing in the hall. She walked down the long hall past teachers ushering students back into classrooms and their seats. Lorraine gently turned the girl away from the departing woman to face a doorway full of students.

"Sit!" she said and pointed toward their seats.

The students scrabbled to their seats, and Lorraine guided Neecey down the hall to the bathroom.

"Pamela?" she called. "Neecey, tell me who's touching you?"

The girl was mute as Lorraine pressed cold paper towels against her face. Lorraine knew that the child had lost all confidence in her teacher's ability to save her.

It would be two more years before "The Battered Child Syndrome" appeared in the *Journal of the American Medical Association*, and even more years before laws were in place to give educators the right to report such abuse. Lorraine Cole would be one of the activists for those laws. For now, she had six hours to nurture her students. Six hours of love. Six hours of safety.

AFTER SCHOOL, Neecey found Ruby in bed, groaning and asking for water. Ruby never mentioned that morning at school, and Neecey, relieved, fed the children mayonnaise sandwiches, helped Odessa and Jack with their homework, bathed Serena, and finally, long after the other children were asleep, did her own homework. When sleep dragged her eyelids down, and her head fell upon her book with a painful thud, she rose to go to bed.

A persistent low moan drifted from Ruby's room. Neecey glanced in the room as she passed it. Ruby lay on her back. Her mountainous stomach rose toward the ceiling. Inside Neecey's own hot, dry room, Odessa sprawled across the bed she shared with Neecey, luxuriating in the brief spaciousness of having the bed to herself. Across from Odessa, Jack snored in the bed he shared with Serenda. Neecey set her books on the bureau at the end of the second bed. She slipped her dress over her head and tossed it in the closet. It fell upon a pile of dirty clothes. Neecey opened the window between the two twin beds. A burst of cold air cut through the odors of dried urine and dirty clothes. The wind sliced through her thin slip. She slid the window down to a bare slit. The burst of air diminished to a small stream.

Neecey, climbing into the bed, moved Odessa's feet. She knew by morning that Odessa's foot would be in her mouth. She knew by morning that the bed would be soaked with their urine. Neecey, with her butt hanging over the edge of the bed, positioned her head in the crook of her arm and slept.

RUBY DANCED IN A RED DRESS that hung in tatters around her body. A big dog rose behind Ruby, leaped over her head, and ran toward Neecey. The dog bared white teeth as big as railroad spikes. Neecey turned to run, but her legs were molasses, seeping into the ground. The dog was closing in on her. She felt its hot breath on her back. From a long distance, she heard Ruby calling her name. The dog leaped.

Neecey hit the solid concrete floor butt first. She stood and rubbed her tailbone. She was awake but still heard Ruby calling her—"Neecey, Neecey, Neecey." In the shadowy room with her sisters and brother breathing deeply in sleep, with a thin stream of winter air seeping through the cracked window, Ruby's voice swelled.

"Neecey!" she screamed.

The pain in Neecey's tailbone lost its prominence to fear. Neecey walked toward the block of light from the bathroom. She flicked on the light in Ruby's room. The dripping bathroom faucet and the tick-tock of the cat clock in the kitchen echoed her own heartbeat. Blood blossomed around Ruby's hips. Ruby's hand clutched the edge of the bed. Her face, riddled with pain, resembled a crunched-up sponge.

"Neecey." Ruby turned her head and stretched her hand toward Neecey. Her small gray eyes were soft with pain. Her fingers played the air like an invisible piano. Mesmerized by the blood and those fingers, Neecey rushed to the bed.

"Ruby!" she cried.

"Dear Laud, help me!" Ruby cried.

She grabbed Neecey's hand and squeezed it. Ruby grimaced and moaned until that moan worked itself into a low groan. Neecey's fingers throbbed. She was sure they would break in Ruby's death grip. A shudder ran through Ruby's body. Her face twisted and moved through an array of grimaces. With one hand, Ruby pulled Neecey down to her chest and with the other hand she gripped the girl's shoulder.

"Go get Sarah," Ruby whispered in her ear. "Tell her I can't move."

Outside the apartment, icy rain drizzled onto the balcony. The air nipped Neecey's bare legs and cut through the coat she had thrown on. Ruby's house shoes did not protect her feet from the icy concrete. Neecey raced across the balcony to Sarah's apartment. She knocked on the heavy door, but her knocks were feeble in the night air. Her teeth chattered and she shivered. Nothing stirred within the apartment. Ruby's screams pierced the drizzling rain, pierced all decency and comfort. Neecey turned and banged on the door with the heel of her foot. No one answered. She banged repeatedly until she was sure that her heel would burst open and bleed all over the door. Lights went on in the apartment.

"Who the hell is it?" a gruff voice called.

"It's me, Neecey!" she called.

"Neecey?"

The small outside light came on and the door opened. Warm yellow light poured out of the kitchen and around a burly man. His thick woolen robe amplified the shivers coursing through Neecey's body. Neecey wrapped her arms around her body.

"What the hell!" the man exclaimed. His eyes were crusted with sleep. A white, dry streak of saliva lay against his cheek. "Sarah! Neecey's out here!"

"Ruby's bleeding to death," Neecey said.

"Sarah!" he shouted.

"Hold your horses!" Sarah called. A woman, all length and

bones, wrestling with the sleeve of her robe, scuttled through the kitchen. She jerked her arms through the tangled sleeves.

"What's the matter?" she asked.

"Ruby's bleeding to death! She can't move."

"Good Lord!" Sarah said, stepping around her husband. "James, call an ambulance."

"Don't you think you better see what's going on first?"

"Man, the woman is having a baby!" Sarah snapped.

To prove Sarah's words, Ruby's scream pierced the night. Sarah tightened the sash of her bathrobe and pulled Neecey into the warmth and comfort of the soft fleece. With a lanky hand on Neecey's shoulder, she rushed to Ruby's apartment. Neecey caught the mild scent of Ivory soap and a stronger scent of cigarettes. They found Odessa and Serenda crying in the hall. When the girls saw Neecey, they let out a wail and ran to her. Sarah disengaged herself from the mess of girls and hurried into Ruby's room, only to find Ruby, face contorted with pain, squeezing Jack against her chest.

"Ruby, let me have Jack!" Sarah rushed to the bed. She pried the boy from Ruby's arm.

"Sarah, something's wrong," Ruby cried. "I can't move."

"It's gonna be all right," Sarah said.

Now the room was crowded with all four bewildered children. Sarah steered Jack toward the girls. "Y'all get back to your room," she said.

"But Ruby . . ." Odessa said.

". . . will be all right," Sarah soothed. "Now go."

Burdened by Ruby's screams, Odessa and Jack sat on his bed while Neecey lay in her bed with Serenda nestled beside her. *How*, Neecey thought, *will I take care of another baby? How?* Serenda began to wheeze and Odessa began to hum. Yet the wheezing and the humming could not camouflage Ruby's screams. Odessa slipped under the sheet and blankets and pulled the covers over her head. Serenda's wheezing became more regular as sleep overtook her. Soon, Ruby's screams were part of the younger children's dreams.

DARCY BANE CREATED A FUSS, a racket, a movement of noise that continued even when her mouth was closed and her body was still. From the moment of her birth to her last day as a member of the Chicago Police Department, she squawked and filled even the largest space with her voice. Even the selection of her name, months before she was born, created a furor between Della and Ruby.

"B-A-N-E. Oh no, Ruby. No," Della said upon learning of Ruby's choice. "Don't that mean death, poison?"

"Ain't this been the death of me?" Ruby replied.

"You can't do that to this child."

"It's Bane," Ruby said. "B-A-N-E."

That name reminded Della of a childhood friend who unwittingly tossed baneberries into her mouth and died within hours. At another time Della tried to convince Ruby to seek a more appropriate name. The women ended up tossing words and names back and forth like a volleyball.

"Ruby, I hope you've come up with another name."

"What would you have me name it?"

"Something good, like Henry, Mary," Della suggested.

"How about Happy?" Ruby asked sarcastically.

"Or Joyce?"

"Lucky?" Ruby sneered.

"George, Helen?"

"Bastard child of a bastard?"

"Ruby!"

"Enough! It's Bane."

Della remembered her uncle coating her aunt's soup bowl with poison after he found out about her and the good reverend. Bane. Ruin. Bane. Poison. Bane. Fatal. Finally the argument dwindled into a compromise.

"Don't hate this child because of that lowlife."

"My mind is set, Della."

"At least make Bane the middle name."

"Okay, Della. Boy or girl, it's Jet Bane."

"Black Poison, Ruby?"

"Ain't wasting no more time on a name for this child."

"As a favor to me," Della pleaded. "If it's a girl, name her Darcy."

"To me she will always be Bane."

"For me, Ruby. For me."

chapter 9

THE MUSIC MAN

*i*N 1961, women swapped their reputations and dignity for measly welfare checks. Snooty, snoopy caseworkers barged through their personal and very private lives. They searched the women's homes for unauthorized appliances, television sets, hi-fis, men's clothing, anything that denoted prosperity, comfort, or joy. Bank accounts were not allowed. Telephones were not allowed. Men were not allowed.

Smart women noted the frequency of surprise visits from their caseworkers and established a pattern. The women camouflaged their homes by day, converting their apartments into barren quarters. They stuffed toasters and waffle irons into the vegetable bin. They buried radios and phonographs beneath piles of dirty clothes. Televisions were draped with tablecloths and topped with big houseplants. Men's clothes were placed in drawers beneath children's clothes or tucked under mattresses. After the visits, the women uncovered the television sets, pulled their Sunbeam mixers out of the dirty clothes hamper, put their favorite Sarah Vaughan album on the phonograph, sipped coffee, and enjoyed their restored dignity.

Ruby's caseworker, a diminutive, gray-haired, shriveled woman with small wrinkled lips, walked through the apartment with a clipboard of forms and an attitude. Ruby was her last case for the day. She wanted to rush through the inspection and get home. In Ruby's bedroom, she looked around at the heavy cherrywood furniture. She ran a hand across the chest of drawers. Ruby, with Darcy suckling at her breast, followed behind her. In modesty, a diaper was draped to cover Darcy's mouth on Ruby's breast.

"Nice wood," the woman said and entered a value on one of the forms.

She quickly opened a drawer, flipped through Ruby's things, and closed it. She repeated the process until she had searched each drawer. She opened the closet and racked through Ruby's clothes.

"There's no man in the household?" she asked as she stooped and peered under the bed.

"No ma'am," Ruby said.

"Mrs. Shade, where is your husband?" the woman asked. Her knees popped as she stood.

"Joliet," Ruby said.

"How long has he been there?"

"Almost two years."

"Oh." She looked at the baby suckling at Ruby's breast. "Well, how did you get pregnant?"

"The usual way," Ruby said.

"Mrs. Shade, I'm here to help you," the woman snapped. "I can cap my pen and walk out of your home now, and you will get nothing. So, let's try again. Where is your baby's father?"

Humiliated by the search, the questions, and the tiny woman who strolled through her home like an overseer, Ruby whispered, "I don't know." Five children pressed against her for food and made it necessary for her to beg for money. She couldn't write to her aunt for any more money. Her aunt's last letter had been direct.

Dear Ruby,

How are you? Reeza's daughter is writing this letter for me. I am
sending you $100 dollars that I got from Milton this month.
Milton been very nice sending you a $100 dollars every month
for Pamela Denise. He says if you need money to come home.
He says he won't send any more money for you and your phony
husband. You know me and Clyde got barely enough for us. So,
if you are in a bad way, you should come home.

   Your Aunt Faith

"Do you know his name?" The woman broke into Ruby's
thoughts.

"Yes, ma'am. It's David Hamilton," Ruby said.

"Do you know where he lives?"

"No, ma'am."

"How can I reach him?"

"I don't know," Ruby said.

"You are the fourth woman this week who can't provide information about their baby's father. I don't understand it."

The woman visibly shuddered and led the way out of the
room. In the living room the children sat dutifully on the sofa.
Ruby removed Darcy's mouth from her breast. She slipped
Darcy onto Neecey's lap and adjusted her clothes. Twelve-
year-old Neecey gently lifted Darcy to her shoulder and patted
her on the back.

"How have you been taking care of these children, Mrs.
Shade?" the woman asked.

"I worked at Primo's Cookie Company before I got too big,"
Ruby said.

"Can you go back?"

"I don't have a babysitter anymore," Ruby said. "The
woman who was keeping the children can't do it anymore."

"Did you pay her?"

"No, ma'am," Ruby said. "She was my sister-in-law."

"And she's probably upset that you had a baby while your husband is . . ."

"Excuse me, but can you tell me when I will get some help and how much?" Ruby interrupted the woman.

"Mrs. Shade, I got to be honest with you," the woman said, looking around at the furniture. "You got nice things in your home. Your children are well dressed and, frankly, I don't see a great need."

"What?" Ruby asked. She followed the woman into the kitchen, where a big black briefcase sat on the table. The briefcase, like the woman, was old, used, and wrinkled.

"We'll help you with rent and food," she said. "But with the state of your home, we will not give you as much as we would give someone else with five children. You will have to sell the television and those electric appliances."

"But I had this stuff for over three years." Ruby looked up at the woman, who scribbled furiously on the form. The woman never looked into Ruby's eyes.

"It doesn't matter," she said as she stuffed the clipboard into her briefcase. "The department gives only subsistence. We are not here to help you live a life of luxury. You'll hear from us," she said and clicked the lock on the briefcase.

A DARK MAN WITH DREAMY EYES, Earl Miller drove from South Carolina to Chicago in a brand-new black Chevy Impala with a G.I. bill and two thousand dollars in his pocket. His sister pulled the roll-away bed into her living room and directed him to the steel mills, where he landed a good job. She thought that at twenty-nine Earl had enough sense to stay

away from loose women with lots of children. She didn't real-
ize her brother was particularly partial to distressed redheaded
women. She had no idea that across a bid whist table he
would meet and fall in love with Ruby Shade.

Earl sympathized with Ruby's woes, gave her rides to the
doctor, put food on her table, and exchanged her children's
run-down shoes for Buster Browns. Earl moved into Ruby's
apartment but refused to hide his clothes from the caseworkers.

"Ain't no criminal, sneaking in and out of doors," he said.

"But they'll cut me off," Ruby whined.

"Throw that chump change back into their faces," Earl
said. "I make enough to take care of all of us."

To prove his point, Earl moved Ruby and her children into
a huge, three-bedroom apartment on Drexel. Life on Drexel
revolved around Earl: Earl's laughter, Earl's friends, and Earl's
money. Life on Drexel palpitated with new delights. Breakfast
to Earl was anything from steak and eggs to shrimp and fries.
A dull day to Earl meant blowing dozens of balloons and twist-
ing them into animal shapes. Earl brought a hi-fi and plopped
Chuck Berry's "Johnny B Good" on the turntable. The children twirled and danced and kicked up such a ruckus that Mr.
Evans the janitor asked them to please keep the noise down.
(Earl slipped him a fiver to ignore the ruckus.) As long as Earl
was in the home, Ruby was easy and the children's voices rose
in laughter instead of tears.

Earl was always the life of the party, the star. The curl of
his "do" rose high above his forehead in a pompadour with the
sides slicked back. One ringlet bounced on his forehead. He
slid and twirled his feet like James Brown, slipping and slid-
ing up and down the hallway while singing, *Please, Please,
Please, baby please don't go,* always ending his performance by

dropping on his knees before Ruby and gripping her belly, which was heavy with his child.

Earl's voice was as rich and full as Brook Benton's. He hooked up with the Excels, a local singing group with a promising career. Sometimes, Earl and the Excels rehearsed until two or three o'clock in the morning. They had gigs in Gary, St. Louis, and Milwaukee. The crowds applauded and gave them standing ovations, so Earl walked away from that good-paying steel mill job because the Excels' success was imminent. Soon, a continuous line of musicians, singers, and comedians moved through the apartment. Soon, Earl had a string of fans who wrote *I want you* on napkins, who followed him to hotel rooms, who called the apartment, and who showed up for rehearsals. All the time, Earl kept saying to Ruby, *I didn't sleep with her. I don't know how she got our number. I thought she came to see Chuckie. Yo mouth gonna drive me away. You got a good man, and you fussing about nothing. I must be crazy to take this bull from a woman with a mess of kids! There're plenty of women that want me. I don't need this hassle. I'm trying to be something.*

Earl was trying to be a star, and at times the gigs were heavy and success almost tangible. But when the Excels goofed, and they goofed a lot with missed engagements or poor performances, there were few gigs. Then Earl drank beer for breakfast, lunch, and dinner. Then, with tears brimming in his bloodshot eyes, he sat at the piano and played sad songs. Soon the piano disappeared. Soon the Impala disappeared. Soon a disgruntled landlord threatened to evict the family.

"Negro, you need to march yo' ass back to the steel mill," Ruby cried.

"Ah, Ruby, how can I do that and sing too?" Earl asked.

"We need steady money coming through the door. This baby is due in three months and the landlord is talking about kicking us out."

"One gig will cover the rent and anything else you need," Earl said.

"I shoulda stayed in the projects," Ruby cried. "At least we had a roof over our heads. At least I didn't have to worry about getting evicted."

"Don't start that mess again," Earl snapped. "I told you I had it covered."

"They gonna put us out!" she yelled.

"Nobody gonna set a pregnant woman and her children on the streets."

Two months later, as Ruby and the children prepared for their day, the fallacy of Earl's statement became shamefully evident when Ruby answered the door to find Mr. Evans and two deputy sheriffs.

"I'm so sorry, Miss Ruby. For your babies, I'm sorry," Mr. Evans said. He was a portly man with a round shiny head. Mr. Evans shrugged his shoulders and opened his palms to show his helplessness.

One deputy, a rotund man with thick curly red hair and eyes that seemed out of focus, thrust some papers into Ruby's hands. The other deputy, a wispy blond, gave Neecey and Jack, who had huddled together in the tiny hall, a weak smile.

"Ma'am, we are here to process your eviction from these premises," the burly deputy said.

"W-w-what?" Ruby stammered as she read the document. "Eviction?"

"Your husband was told, Miss Ruby," Mr. Evans said, referring to Earl. "He was told it would be today."

"Can't you wait until he gets home?" Ruby asked.

"No," the rotund deputy said. "We have a court order to evict you today."

Ruby grabbed her belly and leaned back against the door. "Please let us stay 'til my husband gets home."

"Ma'am, we have a court order to set you out." The small deputy walked past her, into the apartment. "There's nothing we can do."

Mr. Evans shrugged. "You must go now. You should dress and go."

"Go!" Ruby screamed. "Where the hell am I supposed to go? I got five children."

"Please, ma'am, get dressed," the younger of the deputies said. "You must vacate the premises."

Ruby looked at the papers in her hand. She looked at Neecey, Jack, and Odessa standing in hallway. "Get y'all coats on," she whispered and picked up the phone to call Della.

PATCHES OF ICE sparkled in the early morning sun. The cold winter wind cut through the family's coats and clothing. Ruby sat in the armchair surrounded by her belongings like a queen holding court. She rubbed the sides of her large stomach with her hands, raised her legs, and flexed her feet. She put her legs down and squeezed her kneecaps. The children huddled together on the sofa, as far away from her as they could get without leaving the shelter of the furniture.

Schoolmates pointed and sneered at the furniture and household items that rose and fell behind Neecey (who was holding Darcy), Jack, Odessa, and Serenda like a mountain range. The pee-stained mattresses leaned against the dresser and chest of drawers. Boxes sat upon the sofa covered in plastic that was yellowed and torn. Bundles of clothes stood three abreast, like incomplete snowmen. At one point a cascade of clothes escaped from a loosely knotted sheet and fell on the icy pavement.

"Ugh!" a boy cried. "Look at those dirty drawers."

"Man, look at all those peed-out mattresses!" another kid shouted.

"The whole family pees the bed."

Angrily, ten-year-old Jack leaped from the sofa and stuffed the clothes back into the sheet. Eight-year-old Odessa buried her head in her hands and wept.

"Don't cry, Odessa," Neecey said. "Your tears will be ice."

Neecey had long ago learned to block the teasing of classmates. While teachers like Miss Cole adored her, girls either ignored her or talked about her. They whispered about her dense and matted hair, snickered at her half-ironed dresses, and pointed at her run-over shoes—all the parts of her that begged for a mother's attention. Boys teased her, circled around her like Indians, knocked her books from her hands, pulled her hair, flipped up the hem of her skirt, tripped her, and laughed at her chubby legs and thighs. Neecey learned to disappear, roll into herself, look beyond any present time, any present torture.

"Y'all go on to school," Ruby snapped as she pulled her coat collar around her neck. "This ain't no circus."

"This is better than a circus!" a smart-aleck boy laughed.

Serenda buried her face in Neecey's coat sleeve. At four years old it was already evident that Serenda could not adjust to the ugliness around her. Often, she hid her face in Neecey's skirt or sucked her thumb or glanced longingly at the cartoons on television. She could shut out the unpleasantness around her by clucking her tongue against the roof of her mouth. She could shut out the terror that Ruby's voice instilled in her by humming. She learned at an early age that a wheezing attack diffused Ruby's rage against her.

Soon the street emptied of schoolchildren. The wind flew off Lake Michigan, around the luxury Lake Meadows apartment complex, through the shopping mall, across Thirty-fifth Street, and caught the children in an icy whirlwind. Their teeth chattered and their bodies shivered. Some neighbors eyed the appliances, hoping that the family would leave the scene so they could swoop down and tote away coveted items. One of the neighbors invited Ruby and her children into her home.

"If you will just let the children stand inside yo' hall, I would appreciate it," Ruby said. She rose from her throne, placed her hands in the small of her back, and stretched. That same neighbor sent Neecey out with a cup of coffee for Ruby, who held it in her hands like gold.

"Where's Bane?" Ruby asked, peering over the cup. Her red curls peeped from beneath a black and red wool hat. Neecey wondered how she could remain so calm and peaceful.

"Jack has her," Neecey said.

"Good."

"Ruby, what are we going to do?" Neecey asked.

"Don't you worry," Ruby said. "Earl will be here soon."

In response to Ruby's call, Della arrived in a huff. Her small voice rode the wind like a siren. She climbed out her car and looked at the pyramid of belongings. She pulled her fur collar up to her ears against the harsh wind that blew up Drexel, a wide boulevard with beautiful graystones and brownstones. Drexel spoke middle-class success for many of the blacks who had migrated from the South. Evictions were not common on Drexel Boulevard. Della shook her head and looked down at Ruby's red nose and red eyes. Bundles of clothes rose around her on the sofa. Tracks of tears had dried on her cheeks and crusted over. Her teeth chattered and her hands, wrapped around a cup of cool coffee, shook.

"What kinda sonovabitch won't pay the rent?" Della asked.

"He was gonna pay it today when he came in from the Vegas gig."

"I thought he was due back yesterday," Della said and pushed a bundle of clothes back. She sat on the edge of the sofa and wrapped her arms around her body.

"The gig got extended," Ruby said and looked down at her swollen feet in the black flat shoes. Her toes felt like ice.

"Ruby, he knew they were going to evict you today. He coulda told you! He coulda wired you money to pay the rent! He's a snake! A slithering lowlife snake! Girl, I hate to get in yo' business, but you never let Jesse treat you this bad. Why you letting that man dog you?"

"Ain't no spring hen, Della," Ruby said with a sigh. "I got five kids and I'm pregnant. It's hard."

"Still . . ." Della began.

"You got Pete and no children," Ruby said. "You just don't see."

"Ain't this a blip!" Della exclaimed and jumped up from the sofa. She waved her hands around the dispossessed belongings. "You got blinders on, and I'm the one can't see! How low you gotta go, Ruby? How low?"

"Not now, Della," Ruby said. "I got to figure out what to do about my stuff."

"I woke Pete up," Della said and stomped her feet to keep the chill away. "He and a couple of his buddies are gonna move yo' stuff to our basement. Y'all can stay with us until you find another place. But that dap daddy of yours can't spend one night in my house. Not one."

chapter 10

DELLA'S CRADLESONG

RUBY HAD CONVINCING EXCUSES for Earl's failure to appear with cash in hand for a new apartment. The gig had been extended. He had been in a car accident. He was somewhere sick. He was in jail. He didn't know how to contact her. He was ashamed. He was dead. Six days after her eviction, Ruby went into hard labor and gave birth to Jordan Shade nine weeks too early. In the calm of her kitchen, while making lunch for the children, Della tried to reason with Earl's sister on the telephone.

"I don't know where he is!" his sister snapped.

"Listen," Della pleaded as she cradled the phone under her neck. She laid eight slices of bread on the counter. "Earl has a newborn daughter. The baby and Ruby are doing poorly."

There was quiet on the other end of the phone. Della leaned across the counter and pushed the bright yellow curtain back from the window. She raised the window slightly.

"Are you there?" Della asked.

"Yeah, Della."

"Doncha think he'll wanna know about his child?" Della asked as she twisted the top off the mayonnaise. She shifted the phone in place with her chin. "The baby looks just like him."

"Della, he's married."

"What did you say?" The knife laden with mayonnaise paused above the bread.

"He called me 'bout two weeks ago. Said he was married and staying in Vegas. That's the last I've heard from him."

"What about Ruby?" Della asked and fingered one of the slices of bread.

"Be honest, Della. Would you want yo' baby brother married to a woman with six children? That woman passes babies like horse droppings."

When Della was a girl in Thomasville, Georgia, the only clothes that covered her body were made of flour sacks—from her panties to dresses. Such niceties as slips, brassieres, and shoes came only after she was old enough to buy them for herself. Even so, Della had flitted about Thomasville on warm winds, plucking blackberries from bushes, scooping up fallen pecans off the ground, shimmying up trees, digging for crawdads, and skipping rope to:

You can fall from a steeple,
You can fall from above,
But for heaven's sake, Della
Don't fall in love.

But Della did fall in love. She fell in love with the first crisp bite of a new peach, the drifting cottonweeds, boiled peanuts, her daddy's tobacco, turnip greens, her mother talc, the heehaws of a donkey, Sunday hymns, churned butter, and the joyous voices of children leapfrogging around Thomasville. When she yielded her body to Pete, it was all that Georgia love coursing through her body that carried him and her on brilliant waves of pleasure. Yes, Della wanted a child to bridge the gap between her past and her future. She wanted a child conceived in that

Georgia love to sprint around her Chicago home. For seventeen years nothing had emerged from Della's womb but the regular flow of disappointment. Della stood in her big house with her one husband and empty womb and realized that at thirty-six, she had nothing in common with Ruby but a surname.

"You got a niece," Della said to Earl's sister. "What about that?"

"I got my own set of worries," his sister answered. "And Della, if he was so concerned, he would be with Ruby and not married."

Della did not notice the children filing into her kitchen for lunch. She did not see Neecey struggling to hold fifteen-month-old Darcy on her hip. Della heard the scraping of chairs, her name, a dog barking, a truck, a bird, and *horse droppings*. She slammed the phone down. Tears ran down the angry creases of Della's face.

"Auntie?" Neecey said. "Auntie, are you all right?"

"Horse droppings?" Della asked the air.

"Auntie," Neecey tugged her sleeve. "What's the matter?"

Della looked around her kitchen. The oven would never bake tons of tea cakes for her children. The refrigerator would never hold gallons of milk for her children. Della looked at Neecey and had an urge to hug her. She wanted to teach the child about the chambers of a beehive, the razor sharpness of grass, and the poison of baneberries. Della tasted the saltiness of her own tears and wiped her face. *A bunch of babies,* Della thought as she looked into the faces around her kitchen table: Jack, Odessa, and Serenda. Their eyebrows met in the center of their foreheads like Pete's did, like Jesse's did, and like all her unborn babies would have.

"Auntie?" Neecey asked as she walked to the counter jostling Darcy on her hip. "Is Ruby all right?"

"Earl ain't coming back," Della said as she wiped her hand on her apron. "You gonna have to help yo' mama with the new baby."

"Yes, ma'am."

"You know and I know," Della said as she took Darcy from Neecey, "that if it wasn't for you, Ruby would be lost with all these children."

She nodded toward the children sitting around her table. The children were quiet, their eyes wide with apprehension.

"Yes, ma'am," Neecey said and rubbed her empty hip.

Abruptly, Della planted a kiss on Neecey's forehead and stretched her arms out to the other children. Odessa and Serenda leaped out of their chairs and rushed into her arms. Jack walked up to the group and looked into Della's face.

"You're okay, Auntie?" Jack asked.

"I'm all right," she said. "I'm all right."

DELLA'S HOME had the pristine quality of a bacteria-controlled lab. Glass and chrome sparkled. Brass gleamed like gold. Dust free, linen crisp, and orderly, the scent of her home alternated between pine cleanser and vanilla. Breakfast at seven. Lunch at noon. Dinner at six. Bed at eight. Day after day. With that precision, two snacks and hugs and kisses. The children, who knew only the rituals of chaos, wallowed in the luxury of Della's precision and order. They played in Della's backyard and slept in huge beds with soft pillows. They were Hansel and Gretels nibbling at the gingerbread house.

"Neecey?" Odessa said one night as they snuggled in the bed. Serenda slept between Neecey and Odessa. (Della had taken the precaution of swaddling the mattresses with rubber sheets.) While Ruby was in the hospital, Jack slept in her room alone. Darcy slept with Della and Pete.

"Yeah?"

"Are we going to stay here forever?"

"I don't know," Neecey said.

"Do you like it here?"

"Yeah."

"Me too," Serenda said.

"I think I'm gonna stay right here," Odessa said.

Ruby's children would have been completely happy if Della had not forced them to return to school. Two days after Jordan's birth, Della drove them to school. In the backseat Odessa sniffed and whimpered. The crisp handkerchief Della had given her as they left the house was now soggy with tears and mucus. Jack counted the lines that divided the street. Between them, Serenda picked at a scab on her knee with one hand while sucking the thumb of her other hand. Neecey sat in the front seat and rocked Darcy, who watched the sky roll by.

"Let me tell y'all something," Della said. "You can't hide from yo' troubles."

"Please, Auntie," Odessa cried. "I don't wanna go back there. Everybody gonna be laughing at us. They gonna be talking about us being set out."

"But you gotta, honey." Della looked in the rearview mirror. Odessa's watery caramel eyes tugged at her heart.

"Can't we go to school around your house?" Jack asked.

"It don't make sense to transfer y'all until Ruby gets settled in a new place."

"Auntie?" Odessa began.

"Yes, my precious," Della answered absently.

"Can we stay with you?"

Neecey looked at Della's black gloves. Neecey could see Della's knuckles through the thick wool. Della glanced at Neecey, who purposely turned her head. Faster traffic whizzed by the car. The children were quiet and still. They waited for her answer. Della bit her bottom lip and wondered if her desires had been so transparent, wondered if the children knew how she longed for babies.

"Yo' uncle and I would love to have wonderful children like you," she said quietly. "But y'all belong to Ruby."

Jack sighed in the backseat. Neecey adjusted Darcy in her arms. Serenda curled close to Jack and put her thumb in her mouth. Each of them knew it was settled. They belonged to Ruby. Odessa, however, would not concede defeat.

"She says we're just in her way," she whined.

"That's just what mamas say when they get upset," Della said.

"We are bad sometimes," Neecey agreed, "and we make her mad."

"She don't want us," Odessa insisted. "She tried to kill Neecey!"

"Odessa, now you just stop talking foolishness," Della said.

"She says we're just little turds in her way," Odessa whispered.

Horse droppings! Della thought

"Dessa, hush," Neecey said.

"But . . ."

"I said shut up."

Odessa crossed her arms across her chest and poked her bottom lip out. In the rearview mirror Della saw the tears slipping from her eyes. Tiny noises filled the car. Jack flicked the silver top of the ashtray up and down on the door rest. Serenda wheezed in her sleep. In the front seat, Darcy stirred and began to fret. Neecey lifted the child to her shoulder and patted her gently on her back. Softly and slowly, Della clucked her tongue against the roof of her mouth. Neecey knew from the expression on Della's face that Odessa had gotten her way.

PETE'S RESONANT *Hell, naw* woke Neecey from a light sleep. She balanced precariously on the edge of the bed. Her legs were achy. Serenda laid across them. A thin slant of light came through the bedroom door and cut across Serenda's face. Her mouth twitched in her sleep. Neecey sat up. She pressed her hands to her eyes and an explosion of colors happened behind her closed lids. A shadow fell across the door. She looked up in time to see Odessa duck into the room.

"Dessa," she called in a low voice.

"Auntie Della wanna keep us," Odessa whispered.

"You got no business listening to grown-ups," Neecey whispered. "Come back to bed."

Odessa waved a defiant hand at Neecey and peeked out the door. The hall light framed her countenance. Odessa was round, from her head to her bulging stomach. Her fat chocolate face reminded Neecey of a five-cent moon pie.

"They're gonna see you," Neecey warned.

"They're downstairs."

"Come back to bed," Neecey ordered, "before I drag you back!"

"You ain't my mama."

"Dessa, don't make me get up."

"Aww, Neecey," Odessa said as she tiptoed across the room. "Don't you wanna stay with Aunt Della? She don't whup us. She don't fuss at us. Don't you wanna stay, Neecey?" She shoved Serenda's leg out of the way.

"Stop!" Serenda woke and stretched her leg again. Odessa shoved her leg again and squeezed into bed.

"Move over," Serenda said.

"You move over!"

"Sh!" Neecey said. "They're coming."

The girls lay still as Della and Pete's voices came up the stairs. Neecey pulled the covers up to her eyes and lowered them to slits. She breathed the sweet scent of Avon's To a Wild Heart. Della had sprinkled it across the bed and around each girl's neck. The girls were still as the couple's shadows flickered past the open door.

"Where's she gonna go?" Della asked. "Ma'Dear ain't gonna help her."

"Not with two extra babies." Pete followed her.

"Whacha gonna do? Throw Jesse's kids in the street?"

"Naw," Pete said. "But we can't take care of the other kids."

"I see," Della said.

The closing of their bedroom door smothered Pete and Della's voices. Neecey exhaled. Serenda curled into a ball. Odessa sat up in bed.

"We gonna stay here forever," she whispered. "I just know it."

ON MOVING DAY, after all of Ruby's furniture and boxes were secured in an apartment on Marquette Road, Pete loaded Darcy and Neecey into the car along with Ruby and Jordan. As they drove away from the house on Wabash, Neecey saw the small smile on Odessa's face, saw silent tears streaming down Jack's face, and heard Serenda cry, "I wanna go with Neecey."

"Why can't we all stay together?" Neecey asked.

Ruby held Jordan against her chest, turned in the front seat, and looked at Neecey. She casually pushed a red curl from her forehead and shook her head. "You need to stop that foolishness. We'll all be together soon. Just as soon as I get back on my feet."

Even as Ruby spoke, Neecey knew she was lying.

chapter 11

CANTATA

N EECEY HAD A VAGUE MEMORY of life without a baby on her hip. Sometimes, she could see Jesse smiling down at her with his small white teeth. At those moments, Neecey wrapped her arms around herself and rocked. She could hear his voice saying, *Here's a Pay Day for my sweetie.* In those bygone days all she had to do was laugh and play and be her daddy's little girl. But Daddy's little girl was growing up without the shield of a daddy's courage or a daddy's protection, growing up in a house alone because Ruby had discovered a way to beat the system. By day, Ruby was a welfare mama nursing her baby at her breast and dutifully home when her caseworker showed up. By night, she was a domestic worker nursing some other woman's children and dutifully keeping her home.

"She ain't gotta work," Ruby said to Della. "She gets enough alimony and child support to live like Rockefeller. But being a cocktail hostess, she can meet doctors and lawyers, 'cause you know she's looking. But I tell you, she ain't no beauty. Her head is too big and her feet are too long. Ugly ass white woman! And some of those men she drags home, I tell you, are just out for a good time."

It didn't matter why the woman worked. Ruby worked to

raise her standard of living, but the only babysitter she could afford was Neecey. While Ruby worked the system, fear worked Neecey's imagination. Like an expectant father, she paced from one room to another. She propped chairs under the front and back doorknobs, and stacked pots and pans along the accessible windowsills. Creaking floorboards, voices in the stairwell, and the wind shrilling across Marquette Road all fueled her fear. Fear released its grip on Neecey only when Ruby's key clicked in the lock.

AUGUST ARRIVED on a sultry wind that swept up from the Atlantic, through the eastern states, and finally the central states, bringing oppressive heat and humidity. Sticky flies and sticky clothes plagued the residents of Woodlawn. Several fire hydrants mysteriously burst open to the delight of hot, irritable children. Women sat in open windows, fanned vigorously, and rubbed ice across their necks and bosoms. At night, folks sat on their back porches and stoops to escape their saunalike apartments. Neecey spent her time breathing the cold sweet scent of liquid refrigerant. She scraped the crystal from the top and sides of the freezer. She ate spoonfuls of the crystals until the freezer was cleaned.

"Girl, don't eat that stuff," Ruby warned. "It'll kill you."

The Sunday night Neecey's world changed, her head was in the freezer while Ruby and the babies sprawled before the television in the living room. All the windows were up and irksome fans circulated a hot breeze throughout the apartment.

"Neecey, get out of the freezer and bring me a Pepsi!" Ruby shouted from the living room.

Neecey stuffed another tablespoon of ice in her mouth, grabbed a Pepsi-Cola, and walked up the hall to the living room. A blue cast from the television fell upon the sleeping form of Darcy. The girl's white cotton slip was soaked with perspiration. Only a cotton quilt separated her from the floor. Ruby lay on the sofa with Jordan on her chest.

"Again, actress Marilyn Monroe is dead at thirty-six," Fahey Flynn the newscaster said. His bow tie bobbed against his short neck as he talked.

"She was old!" Neecey said.

"Thirty-six ain't old!" Ruby snapped. She scooted into a sitting position and took the Pepsi-Cola from Neecey.

Neecey flopped onto the overstuffed chintz chair and dangled her head over one of the fat arms. She sprawled her legs over the other arm. No matter how she sat, there was no breeze, no coolness against her skin. Fahey transited into other news and Neecey tuned him out. It was too hot to drop bombs. Besides, they didn't have a bomb shelter and President Kennedy wasn't going to let anything happen to the United States. But if the bomb did fall and Ruby died, then she would go and get Jack and Serenda from Della. Let stupid old Odessa stay right there. She would get the welfare checks and take care of Jack, Serenda, Darcy, and Jordan. On Saturdays, they would go to the Museum of Science and Industry. On Sundays, they would go to the Shedd Aquarium. For dinner they would have fried chicken and mashed potatoes with corn. They would sit on the back porch in the evenings when it was too hot to watch Fahey Flynn and P. J. Hoff. There would always be ice cream in the refrigerator and new clothes in their closets. Yeah, and they would buy a house near Della's with a huge backyard, and . . .

"Neecey? Neecey, do you hear me? Answer the phone!" Ruby's voice and the shrill of the telephone broke into Neecey's thoughts.

Neecey dragged herself from her fantasy and padded to the green telephone seat. She turned on the dim sconce lamp mounted above the seat and answered the phone.

"I have a long-distance telephone call for Mrs. Ruby Beasley," a nasal voice said.

"Ruby Beasley?" Neecey asked.

"Beasley?" Ruby asked. "Who is it?"

"Long distance," Neecey said.

"Tell her one moment," Ruby said and slipped her feet into her slippers. Neecey told the operator to hold and dangled the phone before Ruby. The dim hall light softened Ruby's face as she walked to the phone. Her hair, longer and dyed a rusty brown, fell across one eye. She flopped into the telephone seat.

"Hello," Ruby answered the phone.

Neecey stood against the doorframe. She smelled fresh urine and knew that Jordan's diaper needed changing. Neecey crinkled her nose. Jordan would just have to wait for once.

"My God! No! When?" Ruby cried. She pulled her left foot onto the chair and began to pick the callus around her toenail. Her voice held concern but her face was blank. Ruby caught Neecey's eye and pointed to her Pepsi.

"And Faye saw the whole thing, huh?" Ruby asked.

Neecey rushed and grabbed the tall swirly bottle. At the mention of Faye's name, Neecey's attention took hold. Ruby gestured with pointed fingers toward the top of the stand. Neecey set the Pepsi down just in time to see Ruby remove a clog of dead skin from her big toe.

Neecey stood and walked to the stand and listened intently to Ruby's half of the phone conversation. Standing in that hallway, with the fans whirring in every room, the late night traffic swooshing by on Marquette Road, and "Only You" drifting up from the jukebox in Two Fingers Lounge, Neecey wanted to know what Faye had seen.

"Lord, Auntie, of course I'll be there. The children need me. I'll be on the first thing south. I'll let you know when to expect me," Ruby said and hung up the phone. She leaned back in the chair and rubbed her temples with the palms of her hands. She looked at Neecey and smiled as if she was presenting Neecey with the keys to the city.

"Yo' daddy is dead. Got killed by some white man over some white woman."

"My daddy?" Neecey asked.

"Yeah," Ruby said and stood and stretched.

Neecey stared at her, soaking in the word *dead*. That word broke five years of silence. *Dead.* Jesse was dead. Now all Neecey's dreams of Jesse returning slipped away. He was dead like tree bark or old wounds. The earth had swallowed him—whole.

"You never got a chance to know him," Ruby said. "But thank God, that old skinflint knew how to 'cumulate a dollar. Laud, Mr. Milton was a stingy man. You're bound to get a good share of money out of this."

"Mr. Milton?" Neecey asked.

"You remember," Ruby said. "He came to visit you when we lived with Louise and didn't he act the fool. Pulling on me, until Jesse had to beat the snot out of him."

The bogeyman! Mr. Milton, the yellow bogeyman, the man who had followed her home, who Jesse had beat up, was her daddy. Jesse was not her daddy, had never been her daddy. Memories flooded back, and the thunder broke. She was a little girl again, standing behind lace curtains. She was a little girl again, watching her mother struggle against the bogeyman.

"No!" she screamed. Mr. Milton was not her daddy! "No!

No! No!" She shook her head vigorously. A stone crushed her heart. Jesse was not her daddy. He had never been her daddy! She collapsed against Ruby.

"Girl, stop this foolishness." Ruby pushed her away. "Hell, you only saw him that one time. Whacha carrying on about?"

Now the fog cleared. Mr. Milton came and chased Jesse away. Mr. Milton came and hunger gnawed at her stomach. He came and men plagued her. She had no daddy, no daddy— only a bogeyman chasing all the good things away. Now when she looked in the mirror at her dull brown skin and hazel eyes, she understood why she was not a rich caramel like Jack and Serenda or a deep chocolate like Odessa. Now she understood why caramel and chocolate were not flavors in her face.

"Shit!" Ruby exclaimed. "Della! I gotta call Della!"

Ruby left for Mississippi Monday evening. Neecey watched the train roll out of the Sixty-third Street Station and wondered, *Who am I? Is Ruby really my mother? What is my real name? Pamela Denise Shade? I'm a Shade like Jack, like Odessa, and like Serenda. Of course, Jesse is my daddy. Not Mr. Milton. Jesse.*

Faceless men walked her dreams. She woke in the middle of the night and cried "Daddy?" There were no answering words. Jesse. Mr. Milton. Both were her daddies, and both were gone.

"Neecey?" Della asked the third day after Ruby's departure. "Are you all right?"

Neecey tilted her head and thought, *All right? I am not here. I am not real. I am not all right.* The world spun and righted itself. Yes, she was standing in Della's living room with the many children around her legs.

"Neecey?"

"I'm *all* right," Neecey whispered.

A week later Ruby returned home angry with locked lips but no Chauncey, Faye, or Edna. "I didn't feel like fighting," she said to Della. "That's all I wanna say on the matter."

"I'm sorry," Della said. "I know how much you were counting on this."

"Laudy! I spent three hundred dollars for new clothes and the tickets. I ended up with nothing."

Neecey wanted to grab her and shake her and ask, *Who am I? What's real? Why did you lie to me? Where's Jesse? Who are you?* Instead she wandered around with unanswered questions. She wandered into the halls of Hyde Park High School a year early, out of touch with the self-assured cheerleaders, the math whiz, the football captain, the Mary Beths, the Sandras, the Jimmys, and all the other students who were at least a year older than she. She wandered through the halls lost in a dream that could not give her the answers she needed. Sometime after Jordan's first birthday, a red flow demystified Neecey's life. She touched air. She touched water. She touched ground as woman. Of that she was sure. Each month, she had proof.

STILL, SHE TRUDGED THROUGH THE HALLS of Hyde Park High School with her arms wrapped around her blue notebook and her shoulders hunched. Her head was constantly down, as if she found the toes of her shoes fascinating. It was this stance that caused her to collide into Jerome Drake.

"You're just a kid!" he exclaimed. "Whacha doing here?"

"I-I-I . . . ," she stammered.

He bent and picked up her fallen notebook. Her fingers tingled when he touched her hand. He smiled a lopsided smile that slipped past his thin nose and the coffee-colored birthmark on his left cheek. She shivered and caught her breath.

"Algebra?" he questioned and put the book under her arm.

The hall of Hyde Park High School was thick with students and teachers. Neccey felt the touch of cotton, leather, wool as people brushed passed her. Still, she could not look beyond the smiling boy. There was gentleness in his dark eyes. She wanted to stay there in the brightness of his smile.

"How old are you?" he asked.

"Thirteen," she whispered.

"Damn! I barely made it out of eighth grade at fourteen," he said. "You must be really smart."

She said nothing. Smart was only window dressing to hide all that she was feeling. She pressed her notebook and algebra book against her chest. She looked down at her scruffy shoes and his shining Florsheim shoes.

"Hi, don't you live in my building? Thirteen-fifty? Right?"

She nodded her head.

"You be careful, ducky," he said. "Keep your head up."

He was gone as quickly as he had bumped into her. Still in her head she saw his smile, his dark eyes, and heard his warning.

chapter 12

THE COURTING SONG

MANNY STOOD IN THE DOORWAY with a brown bag clutched in one hand and a bunch of wilted-looking violets in the other. His massive feet, his thick trunk legs, and his wide chest reminded Neecey of Frankenstein. His acidic and bitter body odor hit Neecey like a bad afterthought.

Neecey followed Manny into the living room. Ruby sat like a perfect mother in the middle of the sofa with Jordan cradled in her arms and Darcy sitting beside her. On the cocktail table was a pitcher of lemonade and a plate of tea cakes. Neecey thought of curtsying and asking, "Anything else, ma'am?" But she was stunned by the wash of bliss upon Ruby's face. *Omigod!* she exclaimed to herself. *She's pretty.* The hard lines of Ruby's permanent frown were gone. A serene smile played at the corner of her lips. Her gray eyes were dewy and soft. Even her hair, which Neecey had always thought of as plain red, had a copper glint, like a new penny.

"Woman, you got a fine mess of kids," Manny said to Ruby. He stood at the end of the cocktail table like a big hunk of meat. He looked around at the immaculate room. The sofa and armchair, although old and worn, had no stains. Sunlight streamed through pale blue sheers at the window and danced over the armchair. The large room swallowed the furniture.

The bare walls accentuated the emptiness of the room. Even his large bulk did not diminish the size of the space.

"Yes sir," he said, "a real fine mess of kids."

Ruby smiled at him. A tiny, weak smile that said, "Thank you."

Neecey shook her head and grimaced. What was wrong with Ruby? She couldn't like this man. He smelled like rotten rutabagas. His eyes were wide and slanted. His nose jutted out from his face like a protractor. There was a stern look on his face, no nonsense, no laughter.

"I bought y'all some candy." He turned to Neecey. "Yo' mama said you had a wicked sweet tooth. I bought you all yo' favorite candy."

"That's . . ." Neecey began, but Ruby gave a tiny quick shake of her head. ". . . *Jack*," she finished silently.

"Just thank Mr. Manny, like a good girl, Neecey," Ruby smiled.

Neecey frowned and looked at Ruby. Ruby sounded as proper as Jane Wyman on *Father Knows Best*. Her shirtwaist dress, cinched by a large patent-leather belt, could have belonged to Donna Reed. Underneath the dress, Neecey knew a waist cincher held Ruby's flabby, chitterlings-looking stomach in place. She knew because she had pulled and tugged and latched the hooks as Ruby held on to the door frame. Ruby smiled and her small white teeth shone through the bright orange lipstick.

"Thank you, Mr. Manny," Neecey said and took the bag from him. The top of the bag was soggy from his sweaty hand. She opened the bag and saw all of Jack's favorites—Nut Chews, Mary Janes, Bit O' Honey, and three thick Hershey bars. Not one Pay Day was in the bag.

"I bought these flowers for you, but I put them in the back

window of my car," Manny said, explaining the condition of the flowers.

"Thank you," Ruby said in her Jane Wyman voice.

"You deserve better than these wilted flowers," Manny said. "I'll get you some mo'," he said and placed the flowers next to the pitcher of lemonade. The wilted purple petals scattered across the table.

"Oh, Manny, that is so sweet," Ruby said. "Please, sit down."

"Look at this little one," he said. He sat down and pulled two-year-old Darcy onto his lap. The gold and diamond pinkie ring on his chubby finger winked at Neecey. There was an eeriness to the motion of his big meaty hand on Darcy's back that reminded Neecey of Booker. Neecey dropped the bag of candy on the table and grabbed Darcy from his lap. Manny's mouth dropped in surprise.

"Neecey!" Ruby exclaimed.

"Darcy's too big for folks to be holding," she said.

Ruby smiled nicely and said, "You know she's my little babysitter."

"Oh," Manny said and looked Neecey up and down, from the dingy canvas gym shoes to the defiant snarl on her mouth.

At thirteen, Neecey had not lost her baby face or her baby fat. A chub-bug with short legs and hazel eyes, she stood tall and often appeared taller than she actually was. While Ruby adjusted Jordan in her lap, Manny and Neecey faced off. Neecey lifted one eyebrow and silently said to him, *Don't even think about it. Nobody gets hurt here.* Manny smirked. Neecey smiled, a slow malicious smile that discombobulated Manny. Neecey's smile shifted as she looked down at her sister. *Don't y'all worry,* Neecey thought, *I won't let nobody hurt y'all.*

"She's a regular little mama," Manny commented.

"Yes, she do a lot to help me out," Ruby said. "Neecey, take the girls into y'all's room."

Neecey heard a promise in Ruby's voice that had nothing to do with the kindness of Jane Wyman. Neecey didn't care. There was nothing Ruby could do to her. Nothing. Neecey knew in her body, in her soul, that Manny was not nice.

Because Ruby was pretending to be recently widowed, Neecey could not mention Jack, Odessa, and Serenda in Manny's presence. Nor could the children come over for visits. "It's best to wait until I get a ring on my finger," Ruby said to Della. This time she would be a Mrs. This time there would be no babies. Ruby had foam. She had a diaphragm. She had a tired womb. Five weeks after his first visit, Manny and Ruby drove to Indiana and married.

SIXTEEN-YEAR-OLD JEROME DRAKE'S SMILES were crooked and fleeting. Yet, they overshadowed everything else in Neecey's life. Neeccy's thoughts centered on Jerome's thin eyebrows and beak-sharp nose. The dark-roasted, coffee-colored birthmark on his left cheek overshadowed all other images. She spun fantasies of their romance. He declared his love in a field of red poppies. His golden brown skin gleamed as brightly as the Emerald City in the background. (Neecey could not remove this landmark from her fantasy.) They rode the largest Ferris wheel at Riverview Amusement Park. The wheel rose high in the dark velvet night while he gently held her hand. The sky exploded with stars, then the creepy music from the *One Step Beyond* television show would begin (she could do nothing to keep that out of the daydream) and she would hold tightly to his hand. Fear immobilized her. Death was imminent. But someway, somehow, Jerome would save the day by kissing her as chastely as Rock Hudson kissed Doris Day in *Lover Come Back*. Finally, their wedding day arrived. Yellow roses lined the aisle and the altar. Guests as famous as Ruby Dee and Harry Belafonte packed the pews. Neecey marched down the aisle in a sleek satin gown with billowy trains and veils. The rapture cumulated in joy when Jerome lifted the veil to bestow the wedding kiss.

Alas! The fantasies dissolved cruelly as a thirteen-year-old Neecey's face was revealed beneath all that satin and lace. Neecey could not envision herself as an adult. In all her fantasies, she was young and chunky, with kinky hair.

Each morning, she walked with her notebook clutched against her chest toward the viaduct where Jerome and two of his buddies waited, not for her, but for the teenage girls with their pressed hair and plaid skirts, anklet socks, and saddle shoes. As usual, the boys were lighting cigarettes as the Illinois Central commuter trains rumbled over the tracks along Dorchester.

"Neecey?" one of the boys said as he danced in front of her. His hair was filled with blanket fuzz and his clothes were coated with dirt. "Let me carry your books, Neecey?"

"I can carry my own books," she said and tried to side-step him.

"C'mon, Neecey." The boy reached for her books as he walked backward before her.

"Get your knuckle-headed self away from me, boy!" she snapped. "Why don't you stop acting like a fool?"

"Why don't you take your big titty self . . ."

"Hey, man, don't talk to her like that!"

Jerome, shorter but stockier than the other boys, stepped between the two. Jerome's cologne filled her head. She clutched the notebook closer. The boys looked at her. Her usually thick lips were tight and ashy. Her hands were clenched.

"Man, leave her alone," Jerome said. "She's just a kid."

Neecey looked at him. Her lips quivered. She bit her tongue to keep it still. She wanted to tell him that she was not a kid, that she was ten months away from fourteen, that she loved him, that he smelled good, that all she wanted was for him to kiss her like Rock kissed Doris.

"What's going on?" a girl asked as she joined the group.

"Better watch out, I think your man got a crush on the baby," the boy said.

"Miss Humpty-Dumpty?" The girl laughed. She pushed her arm through Jerome's arm and tugged him away from Neecey. "Jerome doesn't baby-sit."

Neecey stood still as the group laughed and walked away from her.

NEECEY SLUNG THE DUST MOP back and forth across the living room floor. Neecey looked out the window at the heavy February snow and knew that Odessa, Serenda, and Jack were playing in Della's backyard, spinning around in the falling snow, catching flakes on their tongues. She sighed and pushed the mop against the sofa. The furniture—sofa, armchairs, cocktail tables, and end tables—was shoved against one wall while Manny stood with a paintbrush and a can of white paint before a fanciful mural he had been working on for two months. His heft filled every space. His large hot dog fingers swallowed the handle of the paintbrush as he lightly dabbed white paint onto the outline of a unicorn. His musty T-shirt was stained with blue, green, and white paint. Bushes of hair hung from his armpits. Manny's odor, that dank, rotten, rutabaga smell, suffocated everything—cookies in the oven, Ruby's Topaz perfume, and Neecey's own Jergen's lotion.

The unicorn and nymphs leaped across a stream flowing from a distant waterfall. Firebirds and a golden falcon careened in a brilliant blue sky. A rank of trees graced the bank. A flight of swallowtail butterflies flew over a cluster of pink flowers. Manny was an untrained talent, so it didn't matter to him that these creatures and plants were contradictions in time and place. He painstakingly painted each detail.

Neecey didn't like the painting. She didn't like the half-naked nymphs upon the wall. Manny had painted the nymphs so that their nipples and pubic regions peeked through translucent material.

The mural, like Manny, made Neecey uneasy. Whenever she walked into the living room, a clammy hand touched her soul and made her tremble. The nymphs had young and innocent faces. Their huge, round eyes penetrated Neecey's heart, pleaded with her to erase them from the wall. The uneasiness she felt in the living room gradually began to overtake her in other parts of the apartment. She wondered if Ruby felt uncomfortable in the room, if she approved of the mural.

Ruby stood in the doorway of the living room. Her natural red hair was dyed black and the curls looked like a pile of dead cockroaches. She cradled the cast on her right arm with her left hand. Neecey knew in her heart that Manny had broken Ruby's arm. She knew it although Ruby claimed she stumbled down the stairs and broke it. She knew it like she knew the bruises on Ruby's face and the missing front tooth were examples of Manny's handiwork.

"Please, Manny," Ruby begged as she caressed the cast. "She got nowhere else to go. She's almost grown. She won't be here long. She and Neecey could share the bedroom and Bane and Jordan can sleep on the couch."

Over my dead body, Neecey thought as she slung the dust mop across the floor. *Ain't no way Darcy and Jordan gonna sleep alone with* him *in this apartment.*

"Ow!" Neecey howled as she accidentally banged the dust mop against her foot. A red slash appeared where the steel clamp bit into her ankle. She hopped around.

"She won't be here until the summer," Ruby said. "She gotta have a guardian until she's eighteen."

The *she* Ruby referred to was Edna. In Neecey's daydreams, Edna's devotion went beyond sisterly love. Edna was noble, a fairy princess. She imagined swapping clothes, combing each other's hair, and whispering about boys in the dark of the night. She imagined all the wonderful relationships from her television families. She had no doubt that they would be the closest of sisters—siblings, friends, confidantes. They would be closer than braided hair. Like Snow White and Rose Red, Princess and Kathy on *Father Knows Best*, and Cathy and Patty on *The Patty Duke Show*, they would share everything.

Neecey ignored the pain in her foot and picked up the mop. She wanted to finish the floor, to get out of the living room, away from Manny and from the tension in the room.

"I told you when I met you," Manny said as he dabbed the brush into the can of paint, "I don't mind children. If you want to bring the girl up here, that's fine with me. I wish you had told me you had another daughter. You lied to me."

"I didn't lie to you," Ruby said, rubbing the cast on her arm.

Manny swirled around and slapped Ruby with the wet paintbrush. Neecey felt the paint splatter against her arm and the side of her face. Neecey, her huge round eyes bulging like headlights, stared at Ruby. The white paint ran into Ruby's mouth. Manny grabbed her hair.

"Ruby!" Neecey screamed.

"You . . . lied . . . to . . . me!" Manny punctuated each word by flinging Ruby back and forth as if she was no more than the dust mop in Neecey's hand. Ruby held her broken arm and tried to shield it from the assault. Manny flung her against the doorjamb and she slid to the floor. He stood over her and kicked her in the thigh.

"Stop kicking her!" Neecey screamed.

Ruby covered her painted face with her arms and whimpered like some lost puppy. Now the evidence was before Neecey—the broken arm and the missing tooth. Manny ruled Ruby with a heavy hand.

"Don't mince words with me," he snarled down at Ruby. "If you want the little gal to come, just say so. How much bread can another one of yo' bastards snatch?"

His eyes met Neecey's. She blanched and took a step back. She gripped the mop and her nails dug into her hand. She ignored the pain in her palm. If only she could smash the mop into his throat. If only she could hurt him.

"Neecey!" Ruby called.

Neecey dragged her eyes away from Manny's face to Ruby, who was pulling herself up from the floor. There was nothing soft and serene about Ruby now. All the prettiness was gone. Beaten, haggard, she climbed up from the floor.

"Clean up this mess," Ruby said.

Neecey looked at Manny again and smirked, a slow vicious smirk that hardened at her eyes. She clenched the dust mop. There was a slight shift in Manny's body, a positioning, as if he was bracing for an attack.

"Now, Neecey," Ruby said. "Move."

Neecey jostled the mop in her hand and walked past Manny, taking in his scent like a predator, sizing him up, and issuing a challenge. *Don't mess with me,* she thought. *I'm not afraid of you.*

DEATH, FOURTEEN-YEAR-OLD NEECEY THOUGHT, should always send warnings—sicknesses, omens, notices through the mail that read, *I'm coming for you. Please advise your friends and family. Please gather them around and say good-bye.* Or, if he must be rude, why not take those people no one wanted. Take Manny, take Booker, take Keith, or Ma'Dear, but not Della, who could wrap her skinny arms around all six of Ruby's children and still have room for more. Not Della, whose words were crisp and quick. Not Della, who looked into Neecey's eyes and said, *This is only a dream, Neecey, only a dream. It will fade.*

Della was dead and Jack, Odessa, and Serenda stood bunched up against the doorway of Ruby's living room like strangers. Ruby sat in the armchair with one hand spread against her face. Manny stood between her and the sofa.

"Naw! Naw!" she cried. "Oh, Lord. Naw!" Ruby bent over and covered her head with her arms and rocked.

"She was walking toward me, trying to breathe, trying so hard to breathe," Pete cried.

Pete sat on the edge of the sofa with his hat on his knee. His eyes were swollen and red. Neecey noticed that his socks were mismatched. *If I didn't lay the man's clothes out, he couldn't dress himself,* she heard Della say in her head.

"Her eyes were so wide and begging me to save her," Pete said. "Her hands were reaching for me. I grabbed her and laid her on the couch and opened up her blouse. I begged her to just hold on 'cause Jack was on the phone getting help. And the girls were scared. All of us were scared. Della kept holding on to my shirt, kept holding on to me and I couldn't do a thing, not a thing to save her. She turned so dark, then her eyes bulged and she was gone."

Time ticked by. The seconds echoed in Neecey's head. She thought the room was too bright for death to be visiting. The sun broke through the window and captured Darcy in a spotlight. The girl stood in the center of the room, looking around at the crying adults and children. She clenched her bottle between her teeth and screwed her thumb inside her closed fist.

"She was gone before they got there," Pete repeated and wiped his eyes.

Neecey heard Della's words echo from the past. *This is only a dream, baby, only a dream. It will fade.* The room spun around and around and Neecey slid down the wall to her haunches. The dream did not fade but crystallized into hard images: Jack bouncing against the wall, Odessa and Serenda clinging to each other, and Ruby holding Jordan in her arms.

"We're sorry to hear about yo' loss," Manny said and dropped his hand on Ruby's shoulder.

"She was everything, man, everything," Pete said as he curled the brim of his hat. "And Ruby, you know she loved these kids like they were her own."

Ruby said nothing. She twisted the ring on her left hand. Manny looked at the three children in the doorway. His eyes raked over the children from the top of their heads to their feet. Serenda shivered and walked over to Neecey and leaned against her shoulder. Neecey put her arm around the child's waist and cried. Odessa leaned closer to Jack, who continued to bounce against the wall. Darcy tottered over to Neecey and leaned against her.

"What do you mean like they were her own?" Manny asked.

"Della wanted to have lotsa kids," Pete said and smoothed the creases he had made in his hat. "Just couldn't."

"Whose kids are these?" Manny asked.

Pete slowly looked from Ruby's bowed head up to Manny's quizzical face. His fingers finally stopped their movement on his hat. The room was filled with the children sniffling as everyone waited for Ruby's confession.

"Whose?" Manny barked again.

"They're my kids," Ruby mumbled.

"Yo' kids! How many damn children you got?" Manny exclaimed. He walked to the center of the room, then spun around. He looked at each child—Jack, Odessa, Serenda, Neecey, Darcy, and Jordan. He looked at Pete and finally at Ruby. "You spring Edna on me. Tell me she coming up in a couple of months and now there's three more."

"You shoulda told him about them long 'fore now," Pete said to Ruby.

"How many more you got!" he demanded. "Tell me *now*!"

"Two," Ruby whispered.

"Two! Nine! You have nine children! From three children to nine children! Hell, naw! Hell, naw!"

Manny spun around and stormed out of the room and down the hall. His voice was stuck on the phrase *nine children*. Pete stood. The grief on his face changed to anger. He ran his hand across his head.

"I can keep them until after the funeral, but after that you have to take them," Pete said to Ruby. "If Ma'Dear wasn't so sick, I could keep them. But with her I got too much on my plate."

"I 'preciate everything you done for them, Pete," Ruby said. "I do."

"And Della wasn't happy about you marrying him," Pete said.

"Della fussed about me too much," Ruby said.

"Damn! Nine children!" Manny shouted. Neecey heard the refrigerator open and knew he was getting a beer. That was the first thing Manny reached for when he was upset, a chilly brown bottle. "So, where the hell we gonna put eight children?" he shouted.

Eight, Neecey thought. *He can't count. Edna makes seven.*

"Or don't you plan on giving me my own kid?"

Oh, Ruby, don't have another baby, Neecey thought. *Please, not with Auntie Della gone.*

THE CHILDREN CROWDED INTO NEECEY'S BEDROOM and looked at her expectantly. Eleven-year-old Jack, with a fresh batch of pimples breaking across his face, sat on one bed. Serenda, who would soon be five years old, stood in the center of the room looking lost and weepy-eyed, even though Della had been buried for over two weeks. Three-year-old Darcy stood next to Neecey. The brown beer bottles tilted against the mirror as Neecey stuffed the wired stems of the paper flowers into them.

"I don't like it here," nine-year-old Odessa said. She sat on the bed with one-year-old Jordan tugging at her shirt.

The radiator hissed. The room was hot and stuffy, but Neecey had firmly shut the door against Ruby, who was curled up in her bed with a blackened eye. Manny was on the road again.

"Ruby is not the same," Neecey said to Odessa, looking at her in the mirror. "She doesn't fuss much anymore, and she doesn't whup me. Sometimes I think she forgets I'm here."

"I don't like Manny," Serenda said.

"I don't either," Neecey said as she picked up a letter, turned, and leaned against the dresser.

"Why you wanna talk to us?" Jack asked.

"I got a letter from Auntie Della," she said. "It was in the box Uncle Pete brought to me this morning. She wanted me to read it to y'all."

"Why she didn't leave it to me?" Odessa said.

"I don't know, Dessa," Neecey said. "Maybe because I'm the oldest. Do you want to hear it?"

"Read it, Neecey," Jack said.

She opened the letter. The children squirmed around on the bed. Neecey walked to the center of the room and stood between the beds. Neecey read:

Dear children,

If Neecey is reading this letter to you, well, I'm not there anymore. You know I love you and I'm watching over you if God allowed me entrance through the Pearly Gates. This letter holds my last desire for you. I know how stubborn you can be, Odessa. Jack, I know you think you're superman, and Serenda, I know you live in a space that's only big enough for you. So, all of you, listen to me.

Once there was a wise man who had seven sons that were always arguing and fighting among themselves. He did everything he could to draw them closer, but nothing worked. One day he called his sons to him. He tied a bundle of sticks together. He ordered each of his sons to take up the bundle and to break the bundle in half. They tried, from the oldest to the youngest, but they could not break the bundle. Then the father untied the sticks and gave them each a stick to break. One by one, each son broke his stick. The father told them as long as they stuck together like a bundle of sticks, they were a match against any enemy, but if they quarreled and fought against each other, their enemy would break them one by one. Remember, children, stick together.

I'm not there anymore, so listen to Neecey . . .

"It doesn't say that," Odessa interrupted.

Neecey flicked the letter in her face and pointed at the words in big block letters: LISTEN TO NEECEY! They were bigger than Della's cursive scrawl.

"'She runs this family better than Ruby,'" Neecey continued. "'Listen to Neecey, Odessa . . .'"

"It doesn't say that!" Odessa exclaimed.

"Yes it does," Serenda said as she peered over Neecey's hands.

"'Stick together,'" Neecey continued. "'I love you. Wipe your faces. Lord knows you got plenty of time for crying later. Aunt Della.'"

She folded the letter and stuffed it back into the envelope. The children sat in silence. Della's words surrounded them. Neecey walked to the dresser. She picked up a beer bottle while slipping the letter under the scarf. She handed Jack the bottle of flowers.

"I don't want that sissy stuff on my dresser . . . ," he began.

"It's for him," Neecey said.

Jack looked in her eyes. Neecey's huge hazel eyes were always kind and soft, but now he looked into hard eyes, eyes like the chunk of dirt he had thrown in Aunt Della's backyard.

"I don't want to be here," Odessa whimpered.

"Manny," Neecey said and paused. She looked at Jack and then at Odessa. "Is worse than . . ." she stopped, not wanting to share the past with them.

"Worse than who?" Jack asked.

"Worse than anybody you know," she said. "Ya'll do as I tell you and we'll be all right."

"You're not the boss of me anymore," Odessa said.

"Boss of you?" Neecey asked.

"Always telling us what to do."

"Always cooking for your bowlegged butt," Neecey snapped.

"Always trying to be our mama," Odessa snapped.

"Always washing your clothes!"

"Always . . ."

"Shut up, Odessa," Jack said. "Aunt Della said to listen to Neecey."

"What do you want us to do, Neecey?" Serenda asked.

"Stick together. Nobody is ever alone with Manny," she said and looked pointedly at Odessa. "Nobody. He beats Ruby. He broke her arm. He knocked out her front tooth. He slapped her with a wet paintbrush and she just took it. If he beats us, Ruby won't stop him. Ruby can't stop him. We got to stand together or Manny's gonna hurt us, hurt us bad."

"He's so big," Serenda said.

"We're like that bundle of sticks," Neecey said as she sat next to Odessa and pulled Jordan onto her lap. "Nobody, nobody can hurt us if we stick together."

chapter 13

THE SISTER SIDESTEP

*N*EECEY PULLED THE KEY off the sardine can and threaded the small tab into it. She held the can over the sink and turned slowly. The thick oil spilled out and the sardines laid tail to body, tail to body. When she flipped the can over, the sardines plopped into the plate, free to fall apart and wallow in the oil. But always, she had to pry the fish apart. It was like that with her brother and sisters.

Jam packed! They were jam packed in the small bedroom. Uncle Pete had shoved another twin bed and bureau into the already small room. Serenda and Odessa shared the bed against the farthest wall, while Jack and Darcy shared the bed right by the doorway. Neecey and Jordan slept in the bed next to the window that overlooked the back porch. Clothes and toys spilled from under the beds, out of the one tiny closet, and from the two packed bureaus. During the day, when they could have stumbled freely through the apartment, they remained jammed together. Their fear of Manny kept them knitted together.

They escaped the apartment through the back door. Neecey lugged Jordan on her hip, Serenda held on to Darcy's hand, and Odessa and Jack disappeared with their new friends. But always, they reentered the apartment as a unit, afraid that Manny would lie in wait for them and hurt them like he hurt Ruby. They could not escape the cries that came from her room. They could not escape the bruises on her face. Only when Manny left for another long haul could the children flitter about as freely as fish in Lake Michigan.

That summer, sixteen-year-old Edna arrived on the City of New Orleans train and strutted into their living room like a runway model in a cream sheath dress with orange and cream swirls around the hem. Edna was tall, slender, and the color of potting soil. Her hair laid around her shoulders like a heavy shawl. She had a hard glint in her hazel eyes and sneered as she surveyed the menagerie of children in their various hues; from Jack and Serenda, who sat around the cocktail table and played Chinese checkers, to Odessa, who sat cross-legged before the television set. She sneered at Manny's mural, which bore additional markings by Darcy and Serenda, and at Neecey, who sat on the sofa before the mural, braiding Darcy's hair. Neecey shivered but gave a weak smile.

"Hi," she muttered.

"Hello." Edna spoke the word ostentatiously, allowing it to convey the weight of her superiority.

"I'm Neecey."

"Of course," Edna said.

Two-year-old Jordan toddled toward Edna with her bottle dangling between her clenched teeth. Taken with the orange swirl on the dress, Jordan grabbed Edna's hem.

"Ugh, get off me!" Edna said and stepped back. Jordan laughed and followed her. Jordan's grubby fingers left prints on Edna's outfit.

"Jordan, stop that!" Ruby said as she set Edna's cosmetics case on the cocktail table. "Neecey, get her."

Neecey lifted Jordan away from Edna. Edna brushed the

hem of her dress and glared at the child. Jordan laughed and reached for her.

"Stay put," Neecey said to her.

"Y'all come and say hi to Edna," Ruby said.

"Is that your baby?" Edna sneered.

A hot flush ran from Neecey's neck to her face. The walls shrank around her. She felt like a jack-in-the-box twisted and bent beneath Edna's hard glare.

"Edna, what kinda question is that?" Ruby asked. "She's just a kid."

"Just wondering," Edna said.

"Didn't I tell y'all to come meet yo' sister?" Ruby barked at the children.

"I see her," Jack said.

"That's Jack," Ruby said. "Odessa is the one with the long wavy hair. Bane is between them."

"Her name is Darcy," Neecey said and shifted Jordan to her other hip. "Come and meet Edna properly."

The children grumbled but rose and walked over to Edna. Edna looked from Ruby to Neecey to the children.

EDNA'S ELEGANCE was her passport into the society of teen-agers that had snubbed, teased, and humiliated Neecey. The girls competed for her friendship while the boys panted behind her like a boar with a rutting sow. She was the mysterious Edna with the soft laugh and musical voice. They admired the ward-robe that she pulled from a bottomless steamer trunk. Where, but on television, had any of them seen so many clothes? While Edna drew friends like electricity to water, Neecey was still an out-sider. While Edna and her friends laughed on the back steps about boys, clothes, and other girls, Neecey flew around the house after Darcy and Jordan. Once she finished holding court, Edna moved to center stage in the family. Odessa and Serenda swayed clumsily behind her and fired questions at her. What color is that lipstick? Does it hurt to pull out your eyebrows? What's the name of that perfume? Edna, bored with their pesky questions, brushed them aside like annoying crumbs on clothes.

Edna lacked sisterly love and offered up no information about her life in Mansdale. Nor did she share any of her memories about Faye or Chauncey. Like a sunken treasure, her past was buried deep inside of her. Even Ruby could not break through her barrier. Neecey waited for her sisterly fantasies about Edna to materialize, waited for those late-night chats and laughter, waited for the swapping of secrets. Spring and summer passed and the moments never came. Edna remained quiet and distant. Autumn inched in and was on its way out and still the moments did not come.

To accommodate Edna, Serenda moved into Neecey and Jordan's bed. Odessa scrunched against the wall, which gave Edna three-fourths of the twin bed. At night the radiator hissed and the noises from the surrounding apartments filtered into the room. Jack and Darcy fell asleep long before the girls' giggling began. Edna, sprawled across the bed with her feet under Serenda's nose, always turned out the light and turned her back to the room. Once she did that, the girls knew she would explode if anyone flipped the light back on. The back porch light illuminated the room. Shadows played against the wall. Neecey, laying at the opposite end, held her hand up so that it was caught in the shaft of light.

"I'm going to have a ring as big as that pink diamond in the Field Museum," Neecey said.

"Girl, Jerome can't buy you a ring like that. Not bagging groceries," Odessa said from the foot of the bed.

"Jerome is going to be a lawyer or a pilot," Neecey said and waved her hand through the stream of light.

"His brother says he can't even pass algebra," Odessa said. "He says he's always failing math."

"It doesn't matter," Neecey said and snuggled down into her covers. "I'm going to be Mrs. Jerome Drake."

"You're dreaming," Edna said and sat up on her elbow. "He's never gonna see you as anything but a fat nerd."

"I'm not fat," Neecey said.

"You're not skinny either," Edna said.

"Why are you so mean?" Odessa asked. She bent her head forward and wrapped it with a silk scarf.

"Y'all just a bunch of babies whispering about little boys," Edna said. "If you had a boyfriend, you wouldn't know what to do with him. Probably play jacks or jump rope."

"Well, I won't let him look up my dress, like Cassandra did," Odessa whispered. "Everybody at school is talking about her."

"Grammar school dummies will gossip about anybody and anything," Edna said.

"Leave her alone," Neecey said.

"Leave her alone," Edna mimicked. "And tell me, how did you get in high school early, 'cause you are one dumb chick-apoo if you think Jerome is ever going to pay you any attention."

"He pays me attention," Neecey said. "And this year, he'll probably take me to the ROTC ball. My dress is gonna be blue with tiny straps. There's gonna be a shawl to wrap around my shoulders."

"Damn! You do dream. He'll probably take your worst enemy," Edna said as she turned her back to the girls and pulled the covers over her head.

IN THE DARKENED LIVING ROOM, the children sprawled and waited for the introduction of *Shock Theater* to waver across the television screen. The television cast a gray light upon Jack, Odessa, and Serenda, who lay upon the blue, pink, and yellow quilt Della had given Serenda for her birthday. In the center of the quilt, the concentric circles moved ever away from a huge, white, daisy carousel. On a separate blanket, Neecey lay between Jordan and Darcy. Edna chose to remain isolated from the group and lay on the sofa. On television, Fahey Flynn and P. J. Hoff bade Chicagoans a good night under clear skies. Bert Wieman, "Winston tastes good like a cigarette should," Hamm's Beer commercials flashed across the screen followed by eerie, screeching, moaning music. "*Shock Theater*" wavered across the screen.

"Go to the bathroom now," Neecey said. "You know you're going to be too scared to go later."

"Yeah, let's go now," Odessa said as she adjusted her nightgown.

"Shoo, this is gonna be scary," Serenda said and trailed behind Odessa to the bathroom.

The living room would be the children's world until *Shock Theater* was over. A bowl of popcorn drenched with Imperial margarine, a pitcher of ice water, two slim sixteen-ounce bottles of Pepsi, and the telephone were on the floor between Jack and Neecey. The title "*Dracula*" trembled upon the screen.

"Neecey, what would you do if you met Dracula?" Jack asked. He centered his elbow in the pillow, propped his head with his hand, and looked directly at her. He rubbed one eye and yawned.

"Sleepy, Jack," Neecey asked. "Or just scared?"

"Shoo. Nothing scares me!" He snapped. "Just tell me what you would do."

"I don't know," she said. "You can't run and you can't hide. He can smell your blood, and if you don't have a cross, you're in big trouble."

"I'd shoot him with silver bullets," Jack said. He sat up and crisscrossed his legs, his thick eyebrows knotted in concern.

"Silver bullets are for werewolves, not vampires," Edna said from the couch.

"Are you awake?" Neecey asked.

"Hmm mmm," Edna said and immediately fell asleep again.

"I'd stomp the mess out of him," Jack muttered through popcorn.

"You have to use a wooden stake on Drac. You take it and pound it in his heart before sunset or watch out!" Neecey shouted and grabbed his shoulder.

"Stop!" He jumped.

"Scared, Jack?"

"Hush," he said. "The picture's coming on."

NEECEY WAS DREAMING. Something heavy was on her chest. Edna was whimpering, moaning. Something moved across her hand. Dracula was now fuzz on the television set. Neecey looked down toward her feet, toward that whimpering. A dark figure stooped by Edna. His massive form hid Edna from Neecey's sight. Dracula stooped over Edna. Drac! Neecey tried to rise up, to move, to save Edna, but she could not. Neecey tried to open her mouth and scream. Everything was quiet and still. Everyone was dead. She tried to move her big toe, to get the blood circulating, to wake up, to slay Drac. She could not move. She had a Pepsi bottle that she could shove into his heart, but her fingers were paralyzed. Wind stirred the curtains at the window and a trickle of moonlight sparkled upon the diamond on Drac's hand.

"I'll make you feel real good," Manny said.

Manny! Drac was Manny! Neecey could see him. She tried to move, to rise up and slay him.

"Come on, Edna," Manny said, pushing up Edna's gown.

"The kids. Stop!" Edna's voice was low and scratchy.

"Just come with me," Manny said.

"Stop," Edna snapped. "All these kids, somebody gonna see you!"

"Ruby won't find out," he said.

"You think I'm scared of Ruby." She laughed.

"Show me you ain't," Manny said.

"No," Edna said angrily as she pushed his hands away and kicked. He grabbed her legs and held them under his arms. With his free hand he tugged the front of her gown. Her breast spilled out.

"Damn!" Manny moaned and touched her breasts.

"Manny?" Neecey's voice broke through her paralyzing fear. Her hand fumbled for the Pepsi bottle.

Manny rose and laughed. He hitched his pants around his waist. Neecey heard the distinctive sound of the metal zipper.

"I was just playing. Heh-heh," he laughed. "We're still friends? Right, Edna?"

"Yeah, we're friends." She smirked and tugged the quilt around her.

Outside the window, red fingers of the sun stretched upon the horizon. Inside gray ash buzzed on the television screen.

Manny walked backward out of the room. He stumbled against the armchair. He hit his back against the wall. Neecey looked from him to Edna, who turned her back.

"We don't have to mention this to Ruby, heh-heh," Manny said. "Right, Edna?"

"Right," Edna mumbled, and with that Manny quickly ducked into his bedroom and shut the door.

"Are you all right?" Neecey asked. "We better tell Ruby about this . . ."

"I didn't ask for your help," Edna threw over her shoulder.

"I know about men like Manny," Neecey offered. "If we don't tell, you might get in trouble."

"I know how to handle Manny."

"Edna," Neecey pleaded.

"You need to mind your own business."

Neecey shivered. *Too many men in the world,* she thought. She turned off the television. She looked around at Serenda and Odessa curled together and Jack snoring in the armchair. He must have moved during the night. She jumped up from the floor and shook the girls.

"Come on," she said as she shook first Odessa, then Serenda. "Come on and go to bed. Jack! Jack! Let's go!"

"I'm sleepy," he said.

"Sleep where it's safe," she said.

A SUBTLE PHLEGM covered everything in the house. Neecey watched Manny's every move. When any of the girls were in the kitchen and Manny entered, Neecey called them out. If the girls were watching television, splayed across the floor with their legs up in the air, like they all did when Manny was not around, Neecey ordered them to sit up. She became the den mother, the chaperone, and the watch guard. One night, after finishing her homework at the kitchen table, Neecey walked down the dark hall to her room and passed Manny heading to the bathroom.

"Good-night, Miss Neecey," he said with a smirk.

She said nothing but continued to walk by him. He grabbed her arm. "Listen to me, girlie. When I get sick of yo' high and mighty ways, I'll put a stop to them."

Manny looked into her hazel eyes and saw the coldness there. Neecey remembered other men, Booker and Keith, using her like she was no more than a rag, using her like she didn't belong to herself. Frost pierced her heart as she stared at Manny.

"Girl, I'll . . ." He drew his hand back.

"What's the matter, Neecey?" Jack asked from their doorway.

"Nothing," Neecey said as Manny dropped his fist. A cold dead grimace move across her face. "Manny is trying to figure out how to sleep nights."

Manny heard a promise in her voice. He saw a gravestone with his name in her eyes. Under the tiny yellow light they stood, caught in their hatred for each other. A shudder coursed through his body. She snatched her arm away from him and strolled the rest of the way to her room.

"Leave my sisters alone," she hissed as she pushed Jack into the room. She slammed and locked the door.

"Did he hurt you?" Jack asked. "'Cause I'll kill him, Neecey."

"No, he didn't hurt me," she said. "Just go back to sleep."

Neecey lay in the darkness and listened to the even breathing of her siblings. She was tired of watching Manny. Yet, she was too afraid not to stand guard. Ruby was a shadow, a ghost of herself with a permanent knot on her forehead. Neecey was thankful that his rage against Ruby engaged his full attention.

Every day after school she rushed home, afraid that she would find Darcy and Jordan's bodies bruised and crushed from the weight of Manny. The girls, so far, were unscathed.

One evening, before Ruby left for work, Neecey cornered her by the coat rack. Under the lightbulb, in the sconce by the door, Ruby looked ancient and haggard. Her gray eyes were dull, lifeless. All of Ruby's former pep had been replaced by sluggishness. She put on her coat like she was putting on a straitjacket. The children were sleeping and Edna was sprawled on the living room floor watching television.

"Why are you still working for Miss Fox?" Neecey whispered as she helped Ruby with her coat.

"You know we need the money," Ruby said.

"But Manny drives a truck," Neecey said and pulled Ruby's coat together. "And what about the money Edna and I get from Mr. Milton's estate each month?"

"Manny pays the rent and the utilities, but he's stingy when it comes to food and clothes. Ten dollars a month for each of you ain't much help."

"You need to be home," Neecey whispered. She watched as Ruby's nervous fingers fastened the mismatched buttons running down the front of her coat.

"Don't talk foolishness," Ruby said. "Whatever is going on here, you can take care of it."

"You need to be here with the girls," Neecey repeated.

"You come up with a way for me to stay home and I'll do it," Ruby said as she removed a cotton scarf from her pocket and fastened it around her head.

chapter 14

CANTATA: WHERE WE ARE ONE

*R*UBY WALKED THROUGH THE HALLS and shouted like a peddler with wares, "Wash day! Wash day!" She placed a large pot of water on the stove and sprinkled drops of vanilla into it. When the water boiled, the aroma of vanilla floated out of the kitchen and up the long hallway. Next, the children toted their dirty laundry from their bedrooms and piled it under the naked lightbulb in the hallway. Ruby, Neecey, and Edna sorted the clothes into four piles. They worked quickly and quietly. Every so often, Ruby would redirect an item to a different pile. She opened her bedroom door and called to Manny several times.

"Please, Manny, I need to change the sheets."

Eventually, he walked out of the room, the belt of his pants unfastened, the zipper half zipped, no shirt on, his chest hairy, and his wretched odor killing the soft smell of vanilla. When he walked through the hallway, he purposely kicked items out his way and mixed the dark and white piles together.

"Manny, we just sorted those," Ruby cried.

"Look, woman, I was sleeping. You woke me up," Manny said. "Just get the damn sheets so I can go back to bed."

Ruby shook her head as she walked into their bedroom.

Neecey crinkled her nose and turned her head as Manny passed her. His odor left a slimy taste in her mouth.

"Be back," she said to Edna. "I got to get some air."

She walked past her room, where Serenda and Odessa were making the beds. In the kitchen, Jack had his elbows deep in bubbles. She pushed onto the back porch and leaned against the banister. The cold December air nipped at her arms and legs. In the backyard below her, a couple of children were making snow angels. Their giggles filled the air. She thought about the last time she had made snow angels. Aunt Della had watched from her kitchen window as she, Jack, Odessa, and Serenda made snow angels in the backyard. Once again, sorrow and longing enveloped Neecey. She missed her aunt's fairness. She missed the smell and touch of her. Della tussled their hair or stroked their faces. Della would make everything right for a few moments.

"Aaaahhhh!"

Edna's scream broke into Neecey's grief.

"I'll kill you!" Ruby shouted.

Neecey rushed into the house to find Edna crumpled on a pile of clothes. She tried to shield her face with her arms and hands. The hall reeked of Manny, who stood in his bedroom doorway. Ruby towered over Edna with a pair of red panties in her hand.

"Yo' nasty ass panties in my bed," Ruby cried, actually cried as she shook the panties in Edna's face. "Girl, I'll kill you."

"I didn't do anything," Edna yelled. "I didn't."

"Liar!" Ruby yelled. She bent and grabbed Edna by her long hair. She pulled her up and flung her into the wall. Edna's hazel eyes filled with fear. She cringed against the wall and held her torn blouse against the swell of her breasts. She tried to cover them. She tried to shield her face with her hands and arms. Odessa and Serenda stood in their doorway and watched in horror. Jack peered around Odessa. His lips were tightened. He looked questioningly at Neecey.

"What happened?" she asked.

He shrugged. "I don't know. I just heard the screams and the slaps."

"I'll teach you to be a ho' up in here!"

"That's enough, Ruby," Manny said.

"Don't tell me that's enough, you bastard!" Ruby yelled. "'Cause I want to know what her dirty draw's doing in my bed."

"That's why you're beating her?" Neecey asked from the end of the hall.

"Mind yo' own damn business, Neecey!" Ruby barked.

"Tell me you're not beating her because of Manny," Neecey said.

Jack touched Serenda and Odessa on their shoulders and pointed into the bedroom. They quietly returned to their room. Neecey walked toward Ruby, Manny, and Edna.

"She's not the problem, he is," she said. "One night, I saw him trying to drag her into your room and she fought him off. He's slime, Ruby. Are you crazy? Why are you taking all of his mess?"

"Girl, don't talk to yo' mama that way," Manny snarled and stepped toward Neecey.

Jack stepped out of the room with a baseball bat and a brown Bud bottle. He sought Neecey's hand and placed the bottle in it. Neecey hefted the bottle and curled her fingers around it.

"Don't touch Neecey," Jack said, wielding the baseball bat.

Odessa, with a rolling pin, walked behind her brother and sister until she was on the other side of Neecey.

Manny's mouth dropped as, one by one, the children united behind Neecey. Serenda strolled into the hallway with a small cast iron skillet. The children's eyes were dead, lifeless. Ruby fell back, stumbled over Edna, who was still curled on the floor, and clutched at Manny's arm.

"You're beating her for nothing," Neecey said as tears filled her eyes. Her jaws were tight and her nostrils flared. "You know he's the problem. He's always trying to touch us. I tried to warn you. I told you to stay home. He could go to jail for what he did to Edna. He could."

"She's lying, Ruby," Manny said. Beads of sweat covered his forehead. His fists were clenched. He made quick, small, downward gestures with his arms, like a jackhammer trying to break through ground.

"Oh, you don't have to tell me that," Ruby replied nonchalantly, waving the whole situation away with her hand.

The hall was still and quiet as Ruby's words sank into the children's ears. She didn't believe Neecey. She believed Manny. Jack and Odessa crowded closer to Neecey. Neecey searched Ruby's face for answers. None was given. Ruby would always pick the man over them. Always.

"What are we supposed to do, Ruby?" Neecey asked, tears flowing from her eyes. She spread her arms but held on to the beer bottle. "Are we supposed to let one of your men be the death of us? Manny isn't going to hurt us, Ruby. I won't let him. If I have to die protecting us, I will. You let him beat you and do whatever he wants to you. That's your business. What goes on between you and Manny is your business. But I'll be damned if he'll hurt one of us."

"She's not worth this fuss," Ruby said and tossed Edna's

panties in her face. "Get yourself up from there, girl. Y'all go on and put that stuff away so we can wash." Ruby placed a protective hand on Manny's shoulder and gently urged him into the room. Ruby entered the bedroom and closed the door behind her.

"What are we supposed to do, Ruby," Neecey shouted. "Die for you?"

MANNY HURRIED BACK ON THE ROAD. His road trips were now three to four weeks long. Still, with Manny gone, the winter winds blew in more tragedy. One afternoon, Neecey walked into the house to hear Edna wailing. Ruby stood in the dim hallway clutching her chest with tears running down her face.

"What's the matter?" Neecey asked as she looked past Ruby, down the hall.

A shaft of sunlight crossed the hall from the bedroom and the kitchen. At the end of the hall, Darcy and Jordan sat at the table with cookies and milk, but they weren't eating. When they saw Neecey, they leaped from the table and ran up the hall.

"NeeNee," Jordan cried and lifted her hands up. Neecey ignored her plea for attention and unbuttoned her coat.

"What's happening?" Neecey asked as she slipped off her coat. "Where're Jack, Odessa, and Serenda?"

"Missing," Ruby said.

"Missing!" Neecey exclaimed.

Neecey trembled. Ruby walked slowly toward Neecey. Her hands rose to the side of her head. She pressed her fingers into her temples and shook her head, slowly, as if to clear away whatever was troubling her.

"Ruby!" Neecey shouted and grabbed one of her hands. "Where are they?"

Ruby gripped Neecey's hands and squeezed. "Auntie Faith called. The army, the government, the country, regrets to inform us that Chauncey, my Chauncey, is missing in action. Missing in action. Chauncey's missing. They don't know where Chauncey is. He's lost somewhere in Vietnam."

"Chauncey?"

"I just messed up," Ruby whispered to Neecey. "I messed up everything."

"Ruby?" Neecey called. "Where are Jack, Odessa, and Serenda?"

"They went over to Pete's for the weekend," Ruby said. She dropped Neecey's hand, walked into her room, and closed the door.

Neecey stooped down to Jordan and Darcy. She pulled them into her arms. "Everything is okay," she said. "I need you to go back to the table until I come in there."

Inside her own bedroom the box of sunlight captured Edna in a fetal position. She rocked back and forth; her hair covered most of her face.

"Edna," Neecey called.

"Go away," Edna hissed.

"I'm so sorry," Neecey said. "Can I . . ."

"You can't do anything." Edna bolted up from the bed. Her eyes were red and swollen and angry. "Get out of here! Just get out of here!"

Coming off the bed, Edna threw punches at Neecey, who stumbled backward from her rage. Neecey backed into the hallway.

"You didn't know him!" Edna screamed. She rushed to the door and slammed it in Neecey's face.

Neecey admitted to herself that she did not feel the loss. She could feel Edna's grief but no sense of loss. How could she miss what she had never known?

POSTERS FOR THE ROTC BALL were on every available space in the hallways of Hyde Park High School. Neecey's attempts at flirting were weak words that trickled from her mouth like dribble: "Hi, Jerome. Your uniform is so neat."

All week Neecey practiced how she would accept his invitation, but the invitation never came. On Thursday, she came home late from the debate club. She slipped and slid through the icy rain. By the time she made it home, the rain had seeped through her coat. She ignored the freezing cold as she thought about changing clothes and heading to the grocery store where Jerome worked. He would ask her today. When she entered the apartment, Ruby and all of the children were drinking hot cocoa and eating tea cakes while watching television.

"Where's Edna?" Neecey asked as she slipped out of her wet coat and rubber boots.

"She trying on her wedding dress," Serenda said through a mouthful of crumbs.

"It's not a wedding dress," Odessa snapped.

"She's trying on a formal," Ruby said.

"It's ugly, Neecey, and she's ugly," Jack said.

"Jack!" Ruby said.

"I don't like her."

"Jack!" Ruby warned.

Jack clamped his mouth shut. His jaws hardened and his nostrils flared. The intensity of his stare frightened Neecey. The venom in his disclosure surprised Neecey. In his light brown eyes she saw anger. Alarmed, Neecey left the living room. She walked down the hall. Jack and Odessa silently followed her. Jack is mad, she thought. He is mad for me. Cold apprehension washed over her. She turned into the bedroom and removed her coat. She tossed it over a chair. Jack and Odessa leaned against the doorframe.

"I could have danced all night," Edna sang and waltzed out of the bathroom, past Jack standing in the doorway, and into the room in a rustle of royal blue taffeta. The strapless gown accentuated her small waist.

"It's absolutely beautiful," Neecey said in a stiff voice. Jack was mad. There was no reason to ask, but she did anyway. "So who invited you to the ball?"

"Jerome asked me," Edna said and turned to the mirror. She smoothed her hand over the dress from her breast to her hips.

"Jerome?" Neecey's heart beat faster. Steam hissed from the radiator, but still she trembled.

Their eyes met in the mirror. Edna's lips were tight and her hazel eyes were narrowed. Could something so beautiful really be so hard? When did Edna turn into stone? Neecey shook her head.

"He asked me." Edna's lips tried to smile, but they slipped into a grimace of disgust.

"But you knew I wanted to go with him."

"He didn't ask you. He asked me."

"But . . ."

"Neecey," Edna turned from the mirror, "he asked me."

"You knew how I felt."

"It's not like I stole your boyfriend," Edna smirked. "I've been here over a year, and he's never paid you any attention."

Neecey felt a hot flush rush through her body. Suddenly,

she was not the beautiful older sister but a rival, a treacherous enemy. Everything about Edna was cold. Her eyes and her voice. For months, Necccey had tried to make her welcome. For months, she had asked Edna about Chauncey, Faye, and Mr. Milton. For months, Edna had been stingy with information, as if Neecey had no claim upon the family.

"You knew how I felt," Neecey said and sat on the edge of her bed.

"Ruby would have never let you go anyway," Edna said.

"Neecey," Jack whispered from the doorway.

"Yeah?" She turned to him. He narrowed his eyes and looked directly at Neecey as he spoke. His twelve-year-old jaws were hard. A twitch worked from the left corner of his mouth to his nostril.

"I saw her in the store all goo-goo eyed," he spoke in a low, controlled voice. "She was batting her eyes at Jerome and whispering . . ."

"You rotten snoop!" Edna yelled.

Odessa looked from Edna to Jack. She saw the tears flowing from Neecey's eyes. She walked past Jack to the bed. She sat beside Neecey and touched her shoulder.

"Don't cry," she whispered.

". . . and he told Mr. Solomon," Jack continued, "that he'd be right back and followed her out the store and down Dorchester . . ."

"That's enough," Edna said and crossed her arms.

". . . and into the courtyard and down the steps to the basement." Jack ignored her. He turned his eyes from Neecey and looked right at Edna. "And I saw them. Down in that nasty basement, with gutter water around their shoes. I saw them."

"You liar!" Edna hissed. Her eyes darted from Jack to

Neecey. Jack's eyes never left Edna's face. Neecey never glanced at her.

". . . she took off her panties and stuffed them in her pocket. Raised her dress and her coat up to her butt and it was cold. Neecey, my hands were freezing, but . . ."

"Don't say another word," Edna warned.

". . . she didn't care. It was cold, but she was standing there with her butt showing and he was banging into her."

"It's all true," Neecey whispered. "I believed in you. I thought Manny was lying."

"Shut up, you," Edna warned.

"You probably led Manny on. You were in Ruby's bed with Manny."

"Shut up!"

"You could do this 'cause you're worse than a liar. You're a slut."

Edna rushed across the room in a blue blur. She punched Neecey in the face. Neecey's head snapped back. Odessa shoved Edna and she landed on the other twin bed.

Edna bounced up and grabbed a handful of Neecey's hair. Neecey screamed as Edna managed to lock her hand into Neecey's hair and tugged. Odessa grabbed Edna's hair and yanked her back. As Edna came up, she brought Neecey with her. Her mouth snarled around her teeth as she jerked Neecey's hair back and forth. Neecey closed her eyes in pain.

"What's going on back there?" Ruby's voice traveled from the living room, down the long hall.

"They're fighting! They're fighting!" Serenda shouted as she entered the bedroom. Three-year-old Darcy trailed behind her.

Edna flung Neecey away from her. She clawed at Odessa's hands. Her long pink nails dug into the smaller girl's flesh. Odessa wailed and released Edna's hair. Jack grabbed Edna's left arm. As Edna turned, her fist caught him on the chin. He fell back. Serenda caught him. Jack flew into Edna again.

"Serenda and Bane better not get hurt in there," Ruby called as she went past their room.

"Edna, stop!" Serenda screamed and charged head first into Edna. The blow shook Edna and allowed Neecey an opportunity to wrap Edna's hair around her hand. Serenda leaped on Edna's back and sank her teeth into her neck. Edna clamped her teeth on Neecey's arm. Through all the commotion, Neecey heard water running in the kitchen, heard Darcy's cries, and even heard her own heartbeat. Odessa kicked Edna and Edna kicked Neecey. Neecey jumped back but held on to her hair. She felt blood and saliva running down her arm. With her left hand she threw a clumsy punch to Edna's jaw. It connected.

"Neecey!" Darcy screamed as she pelted Edna with tiny blows. "Leave Neecey 'lone!"

"Acting like a bunch of heathens!" Ruby shouted from the doorway.

She dashed a large pot of cold water onto the mass of children. They shrieked and fell away from each other. Odessa and Serenda wiped the water from their faces with their hands. Jack used his shirttail. Shocked, Darcy wailed and clung to Neecey.

"Fighting!" Ruby said. The stockpot dangled at her side and a small puddle of water ran under her bare feet. "Ain't never known y'all to fight each other."

"I hate you! I hate you!" Edna screamed. "I hate all of you."

The bewildered children tried to catch their breath. Odessa and Jack stood close to Edna and wished that she would move just one inch. It wouldn't matter about the water that flowed down their faces. It wouldn't matter that Ruby stood in the doorway screaming, *Cows fighting up in my house.* They would jump her if she budged. Jack's eyebrow lifted in a dare. Odessa clenched her fist. Serenda joined Darcy around Neecey. Neecey pushed her wet hair out of her eyes and looked directly at Edna. The taffeta dress was streaked with water. Her hair hung around her head like weeds. Her lips were swollen and her face marred with scratches. There was nothing elegant about Edna at this moment. Neecey smiled.

"You better pray," she said, "that we never hate you."

chapter 15

THE MARRIAGE LULLABY

SLOE-EYED JEROME. Jerome with the coffee-colored birthmark on the left side of his face. Jerome swaggered by their window doo-whopping, catcalling, and talking sweet, and Neecey listened. His voice rose above the speeding cars and the hum of people moving along Marquette Road. Neecey snatched fireflies from the night and piled their shimmering bellies into a mound. She sprinkled that mound over Jerome. Along Marquette Road people paused to watch the cascade descend upon him. Her love sparkled from her hands: glitter, moonbeams, love. Yet, it was Edna in the living room window who Jerome was serenading. Neecey, squeezing a pillow against her chest, rocked and cried and watched from Ruby's bedroom window.

Jerome came up to the apartment polite, but not meek or begging. With a crooked smile he looked Ruby in the eyes and point-blank told her, "Edna and I are going to the Regal this Saturday to see James Brown. I'll get her home about ten or eleven."

Now, there was only a pillow to smother Neecey's cries while Jerome scaled Edna's thick hair and rescued her from Ruby's tower. Edna's dusk curfew went skittering down

Marquette Road, into Jackson Park, and finally moseyed into Lake Michigan.

> *Edna and Jerome sitting in a tree,*
> *K - I - S - S - I - N - G*
> *K - I - S - S - I - N - G*
> *First comes love, then comes marriage*
> *Then comes Edna with a baby carriage.*

BEFORE THE INK COULD DRY on their high school diplomas, Edna and Jerome married and moved into a kitchenette apartment on 63rd and Dorchester. By January it was common knowledge that Jerome was cheating on her. When Neecey saw Jerome walking hand in hand with a girl who was not his wife, she wondered why she had been so heartbroken over him. She sighed with relief that she wasn't the one pregnant and trudging through the winter in a gray coat that fitted like a tent. Often, Jerome dropped Edna off at Ruby's so he could go out with his friends.

"Take me with you," Edna would beg him.

"You're too big to take anywhere," Jerome said. "Look at yourself."

As eighteen-year-old Edna ballooned in her pregnancy, Neecey's fatty flesh curved into firm breasts and eye-catching thighs and legs. While Edna's nose spread and her skin became blotchy, Neecey's complexion remained dewy, soft, and acne-free. Although the newness of her body caused appreciative glances from the boys around her, it did not add to her confidence. She still shied away from boys with crushes on her. Those crushes did not help her forget that Edna had stolen her one great desire.

Often, Neecey found Edna curled on the Ruby's sofa with eyes bloodshot from weeping. Although neither Edna nor Neecey apologized for their past animosity, they drifted into a peaceful coexistence. How could Neecey hold a grudge against someone in such misery? Hadn't Edna saved her from Jerome? Although, according to Ruby, Jerome was a "good man."

"Man like Jerome ain't gonna take no stuff, gal," Ruby advised Edna. "He's a strong man, not one of those you can tie up in apron strings. So don't be nagging. Don't be trying to break his spirit. Horses you break. You best learn early: if you gotta fuss, make sure you got something to fuss about. A man will leave a nagging woman quicker than he will a filthy woman."

Edna followed Ruby's advice, but Jerome still walked out of their apartment to anywhere, everywhere away from Edna. She spent a lot of time walking, looking for Jerome. One night Edna dragged Neecey with her. They checked out two pool halls, a hamburger joint, and finally a tip led them into Two Fingers and found him leaning into some woman; his hands cupped her behind while his tongue flickered around her lips.

"Come on, Edna," Neecey said as she pulled her arm.

Edna jerked her arm from Neecey. Her mouth was dry and ashy. Her eyes filled with tears and became soft, languid, sad things. All eyes were on them.

Music rushed from between the crisscrossed silver arms covering the speaker of the jukebox and spread out like a rude yawn. Cigarette butts and peanut shells on the floor led a path from the door to Jerome. Edna brushed past Neecey. As she walked through the lounge, the hushed crowd parted like hair.

"Edna." Neecey hastened behind her. "Edna, don't start nothing."

"Hey, 'Rome, yo' children looking for you." The woman laughed as if Jerome was her man, her right.

Jerome reeled back, his eyes red. "What the hell y'all doing here?"

"You said you'd be right back." Edna sounded weak, feeble.

"Go home, Edna," he said.

"I'm not sitting at Ruby's while you run the street!"

"Neecey, take her home," he said and reeled back to Mavis.

"Come on, Edna," Neecey said.

"No! I'm not moving!"

"I said take your ass home," he said over his shoulder.

A second is a brief blink of the eye. Neecey saw the next few seconds in slow motion. Edna's hand curled around a brown Bud bottle sitting on the table. Her hand arched high. The bottle crashed against Jerome's head. Jerome fell against Mavis. Mavis screamed as he slumped to the floor.

"You can have him, now," Edna said to Mavis. "Let's go, Neecey."

AFTER EDDIE'S BIRTH, Ruby became Jerome's champion. "He's a good man. Ain't never seen a man so taken with a child. Man like Jerome hard to come by. You better get that chip off yo' shoulder and try to have something with him."

Jerome tossed six-month-old Eddie up to the ceiling and caught him as he sailed down.

"He's too young for that," Edna said.

"He's my child."

Jerome tossed Eddie up many, many times and Eddie always tumbled back, giggling, into Jerome's arms.

"Taking my boy to the zoo," Jerome said.

"He's too young for that," Edna said.

Jerome took six-month-old Eddie to Brookfield Zoo and pointed out long-necked, long-nosed, wide-foot, scaly, and slippery animals. Eddie, too young to understand anything more than the sound of his daddy's voice, cooed and grabbed his daddy's face.

Rock-a-bye baby
In a treetop.
When the bough breaks,
The cradle will
Drop.

On a sweltering night in August, Edna, Jerome, and Eddie slept fretfully next to the open window in their hot apartment. It was so hot flies wobbled through the air and asphalt melted the soles of shoes. Eddie crawled over the bodies of his sleeping parents and out the window. But Jerome was not below to catch him. Somebody screamed like a madman and woke up Edna and Jerome. Edna and Jerome looked for Eddie, but Eddie lay on the ground below. No longer their child, but always their child.

WHEN SIXTEEN-YEAR-OLD NEECEY saw the older men standing by the liquor store on the corner of Blackstone, some inner antennae bristled. She rubbed her left arm. The men were busy with their shake-and-bake mixture, Kool-Aid soft drink shaken in Gallo's white port. In the midst of the men, with matted hair and stained wrinkled clothes, was Jerome, doing the shake-and-bake with a bunch of old winos. He was no longer the immaculate Jerome dressing sharp as a tack. His double-knit sweaters sagged from the shoulders. His cracked and wrinkled leather coat, which he wore even in warm weather, dipped and drooped. Some days he combed his thick Afro, but more often his hair was matted with lint, dirt, and Afro-Sheen. The rancid aroma of dried urine and musk surrounded him.

"Damn! Is that you, Miss Neecey?" Jerome recognized her.

"I'm in a hurry, Jerome," she said as she quickly walked passed him.

"Baby," another man called, "you're looking good."

When a woman knows she's looking good, she needs no catcalls or whistles of appreciation. Neecey knew she looked good as she walked across Sixty-third Street in green-, brown-, and orange-striped bell-bottoms. Her green polyester blouse with ruffles around the cuffs and tumbling down her chest matched the green stripes of her pants. Her wide brown belt emphasized her curves. Large gold hoop earrings accentuated her short Afro and bright green shades hid her wide gray eyes. She had sprouted up and slimmed down.

"Neecey, wait up!" Jerome called.

Neecey stopped and turned. He pimp walked toward her, but his old strut was ineffectual. His face was haggard. The cocoa birthmark was dull and hidden beneath the wild hairs of his beard.

"'Rome," she said.

"Girl," he said, looking at her flawless skin and her full lips. "If I hadda known you was going turn out so fine . . ."

"Don't start no bull with me," she said.

"Cold! Y'all Beasleys are the coldest women," he snapped.

"Don't jump all over my case," she snapped and turned to walked away.

"Man, you don't know what to do with that fox. Give her to me," one of the winos said.

"Come on, Neecey," he said. "You know you're my ace."

"Make it plain, Jerome," she said.

"All I need is five to hold me until Friday."

"Man, you think I got bookoos of money," she said.

"Don't square up, Neecey."

"I got two."

"Three."

"This isn't Maxwell Street!" she snapped. "Two fifty. Take it or leave it."

"Cool."

Neecey watched him scurry back to his buddies like a rat with a piece of cheese. She shook her head and walked underneath the viaduct as a train rumbled overhead. The rumbling blended with the discord inside her. Jerome was caught in a net of guilt and gulping Gallo like water.

EDNA WORKED AT A CATALOG HOUSE for sixty-eight dollars a week before taxes. (Jerome was always too drunk to work.) Edna ran back and forth along the aisles named for states: eight aisles, eight states, eight hours. Her relief came on those Friday evenings when she and Neecey indulged in the stage shows at the Regal Theater on Forty-seventh Street: Mary Wells, Wilson Pickett, Martha and the Vandellas.

One Friday evening, when Neecey went to pick up Edna, she found the door half opened and the curtains billowing across the unmade bed in the kitchenette apartment. Cold air and the prevailing odor of Old Spice cologne surrounded her. She rubbed her hands up and down her arms. The second thing she noticed was the rubbish on the floor. And finally, she saw the open and empty bureau drawers.

"Edna, Jerome?" Neecey called. There was no answer.

Neecey shivered as she pulled her jacket around her. A blast of cold air hit her in the face. The window was hoisted. Although the kitchenette was on the top floor, the fire escape ran adjacent to the window. Any desperate thief could climb from the street or down from the roof.

Another cold blast of air came through the window. Neecey ignored the rubbish on the floor and rushed to close it. The cold and wet of the day had frozen the window in place. Neecey dragged one of the pink chairs from the table to the window. As she stood on the chair and struggled to push the window down, an el rumbled into the Dorchester station. The train slowed, then halted. She leaned precariously forward. She caught the stare of a man on the el. He smiled and winked at her. She pushed the top of the window down with great force. The window plummeted into its frame.

As she walked back to the kitchen area, she noticed that the bathroom door was partially opened. Jerome sat on the closed toilet seat holding a straightedge razor under running water. She pushed the door open. The stench of beer and urine rushed out. Jerome did not look around but stared at the water splashing over the blade. If despondency could take shape, it was in the form of Jerome's slumped body or his drooping head.

For a moment, Neecey was not sure if the rushing sound in her ears was the el clamoring along Sixty-third Street or her own fears. She heard everything—the el, the water, her heartbeat, and Jerome's raspy breath lifting his burdens up to the water faucet. If fear could be described, it was the knot in her throat. She eased into the room.

"Jerome," she whispered.

He didn't answer. Didn't move.

"Jerome," she called again, "what's wrong?"

"Edna's gone," he said.

"Gone, where?" she asked.

"Just gone."

"Come on, let me fix you some coffee," she said soothingly.

"Don't want any damn coffee. You think I'm drunk. You think I'm sick. You don't know Neecey, don't know. My boy crawled over my chest," he cried, and pounded his chest, "crawled right over this chest and I didn't feel a thing. Now Edna's gone."

"Let me have the razor, Jerome." Neecey eased into the bathroom. The sound in her head grew louder. She realized it was her breathing, her heartbeat.

"Why, Neecey? Why didn't I feel him? Maybe I can't feel. Maybe I could cut through my skin and not feel a thing." He flicked the razor back and forth under the water. "Maybe I could slice my own neck and not feel anything."

"You got feelings, Jerome. I know you got feelings."

"Naw."

"Gimme the razor, 'Rome." She beckoned with her hands.

"Can't do that, Neecey," he said. "Gotta see what it takes to make me feel. Gotta know, Neecey."

"Please, 'Rome, give me the razor."

Jerome moved his left hand into the water and brought the razor down. In a flash, Neecey snatched his hand. For a moment she thought she was too late as blood spattered over their hands. Then she realized it was her hand, not his, that the razor had sliced.

NEECEY MARCHED WITH the graduating class of '66 with her throbbing hand swaddled in bandages and her aching feet encased in white pumps. "Pomp and Circumstance" moved her not to tears but pain as the pumps pinched her toes. She wanted it over: the diploma in her hand, the tassel tucked away in the yearbook, and high school packed away like all other memories. When the high school doors closed, summer flew. She was seventeen years old, enrolled in the University of Chicago. Jerome was gone, signed up for the army, and Edna was flying around with some sugar daddy in a Cadillac like Jerome never existed, like he didn't almost die the day he cut her hand, like he didn't cry and beg everybody—Edna, Ruby, Jack, Neecey, and even Manny—for forgiveness. Like Neecey couldn't hear Jerome's sorry song over and over in her head.

Sorry. Didn't mean to hurt Neecey. Would never hurt Neecey on purpose. Sorry, Jack. You know she's my girl. Always in my corner. Sorry. Didn't mean to mess up everything. Didn't mean to mess up my life. Sorry about Edna. Sorry about Eddie. I'll sorry myself into the army. I'll sorry myself into Vietnam. I'll come home all maimed and lame and spend the rest of my sorry days with my mama. I'm sorry. So sorry.

chapter 16

JESSE'S LAMENTATIONS

*R*UBY AND MANNY moved the gaggle of children into a house in an area called The Pocket. This area was bordered by the Illinois Central railroad tracks in the east, Seventy-first Street in the south, and Oakwood Cemetery in the north and west. The bilevel house consisted of three bedrooms on the upper level, a kitchen/dining area and a living room on the main level, and a large recreation area, a bedroom, and a bath in the basement. When Manny was on the road, Neecey fluttered in and out of the house and around the University of Chicago free and easy. When Manny was on the road, she flitted across town to DePaul University and cheered the Blue Demons on to victory. She flew farther north to Loyola University and shouted the Ramblers on to glory. When Manny was away, the girls were safe and Neecey could be a college student immersed in the ivy walls of UC library— reading Bellow, Rand, Trollope, and Sartre.

When Manny was home, she grounded herself in the house and weighed her limbs down with protectiveness. She studied at the kitchen table until the wee hours of the morning. She watched the small hallway at the top of stairs for any appearance by Manny, and each time he ventured out of his bedroom, she was there with a smirk. When Neecey turned eighteen, Manny began the *move* opera that would continue for the next four years.

"Grown gal need to move, Ruby," Manny sang.

"I know," Ruby simpered.

"I'm still in school," Neecey descanted.

She was a twenty-one-year-old public policy major with acceptance letters from graduate schools across the country, but she could not fly away to New York or California and leave the girls in the lecherous paws of Manny. Odessa was the first to escape the house. She found religion in a Lutheran church and finagled a scholarship to a Lutheran boarding school in South Dakota. Jack made his escape to Howard University and an internship at the *Washington Post*. Yet there still remained three fledglings under the neglectful eye of Ruby. Those three fledglings were blooming, and Manny still eyed them like lollipops. If Neecey left, who would protect thirteen-year-old Serenda, eleven-year-old Darcy, or ten-year-old Jordan from Manny?

"Get out," Jack wrote from Howard University.

"I will, I will, I will," she said to herself. "But not now. Not now. I can't leave the wolf in the henhouse. No, I don't think so."

Still, *move* became a living, breathing word that emanated from the walls as Neecey moved through the house. Her footsteps caused the floorboards to groan *move*. Her hand on a switch caused the light to squeal *move*. The two flights of stairs leading up and down, the nine heavy wooden doors, the two drippy faucets, every window in every room, the cheap prints on the walls, the shag carpeting, the canopied beds and bunk beds, the plates, spoons, dustpan, banister, and even the drain screamed *move*. The house was a choir. Its members, from the deep bass section of the basement to the high sopranos in the bedroom, sang out in quick staccato beats—*move-*

move-move-move-move-move—and Neecey studying at the kitchen table, dressing in the cold basement bedroom, ironing in the kitchen, found herself humming: mmm-mmm-mmm-mmm-mmm-mmm, like a hurt child.

In the summer of 1971, with Odessa and Jack home from their respective schools, the family gathered in Ruby's house, not realizing that this would be the last summer they would be together, the last time until death brought them together years later. Sunlight filtered through the crisp yellow curtains at the kitchen window. A planter of ivy trembled from the breeze through the crack in the window. An overwhelming aroma of fried catfish filtered throughout the bilevel home. Neecey sat at the imitation French provincial dining room table set with her back to the stairs leading up to the second floor and the set of stairs leading to the basement. She swirled chocolate around a three-layer cake. Odessa sat across the table from her with lettuce, radishes, red onions, and raspberries. As she tore the lettuce into pieces, she tossed them into a large pottery bowl on the table. Ruby walked from the refrigerator to the counter with a carton of Parmesan cheese. Edna, in high-heeled red suede boots and a pomegranate red derby to match her pomegranate red jumpsuit, leaned against the side of the refrigerator. Her huge Afro mushroomed around her head like a nuclear explosion. As she talked, she jabbed an unlit Tiparillo. Behind Edna, on the opposite side of the wall, Jack leaned over the stereo, sorting through albums and singing along with "Groovin'" by the Rascals. His dark shirtless body glistened with sweat. A wide-brim black Dobbs covered his unpicked Afro. He was waiting patiently for his turn on the Monopoly board.

In the center of the room Jordan swayed to the music. Jordan's yellow skin was dulled and dingy, and her red Afro was matted to her head. Serenda and Darcy sat on each side of the cocktail table. In front of them, the Monopoly board was loaded with houses and hotels. Serenda, with skin as buttery and rich as toffee and Afro puffs on each side of her head, bent forward and rolled the dice. Darcy, whose skin was so dark that it looked iridescent in sunlight, crossed her fingers. Her short Afro was a dirty brown, the same color as her small eyes.

"Yes!" Serenda exclaimed.

"We're in trouble," Darcy said. "She's just got Marvin Gardens."

"I quit," Jack said.

"That cheating," Darcy said.

"Yeah," said Jordan. She flopped on the floor before the table.

"Sue me," Jack said as he rose from the stereo.

"And it looks like I'm getting a four-year scholarship to the college," Odessa said. She was the only female in the house with relaxed hair. Even Neecey and Ruby sported short Afros.

"Gotta call from Miss Lula," Edna said, interrupting Odessa. "She said Faye's back in Mansdale and sick in the head."

"Faye got more sense than Einstein," Ruby said as she vigorously shook the cheese over a huge bowl of spaghetti. Her hair, naturally red again, had spots of gray. Over the years she had thickened into a wide woman with hips that bowed from her body like a hoop skirt.

Edna jabbed the unlit Tiparillo toward Ruby as she yakked about Faye and Miss Lula. Neecey caught snatches of the rant. "Had to . . . I couldn't run down there . . . my store opening . . . Faye . . . take it slow and easy . . . Miss Lula wouldn't get off the phone . . . your number."

"Odessa, I'm coming for your graduation next year," Neecey said, interrupting Edna's jabbering.

"Really?" Odessa asked.

"Yeah," Neecey said. "Somebody should have visited you long before now."

"Geez, Neecey, it's okay," said Odessa. She raised one eyebrow and looked directly at Neecey. "It's really okay."

Neecey gave her a quick quirky smile that said, *I understand, I catch your drift, I know what you mean.* Odessa did not want her family coming to that boarding school in the middle of the prairie. Neecey, knowing Odessa and Odessa's snobbery, imagined her walking across that campus with her hair flowing and her voice, crystal clear and missing any South Side Chicago dialect, tinkling, pretending that her family were wealthy sophisticates. Neecey knew Odessa was pleased that Ruby could never make open house or family day or any of the other events the school sponsored throughout the year. Neecey licked chocolate from the spatula and rose from the table.

"Get used to the idea," she said. "I'm coming."

"Alone?"

"Well, you don't expect me to fly halfway around the world just to see you graduate high school?" Ruby snapped as she brushed passed Neecey with the bowl of spaghetti. She set the bowl in the center of the table.

"Alone." Neecey smiled and walked to the sink with the bowl.

"I know you're busy," Odessa said as she tossed raspberries on top of the spinach and red onions. "Neecey can take a bunch of pictures."

"Each day through my window, I watch her as she passes by . . ." Jack's voice floated from the living room as he sang along with the Temptations.

"Jack, you're no Temptation," Edna called as Jack hit an unnerving note.

"And you're no fashion queen," he answered.

Neecey looked out the kitchen window to the huge three-story white frame house next door. She poured herself a cup of coffee from the coffeemaker and returned to the table.

"You talked to Jerome's mama?" Ruby asked. She carried a large platter of garlic bread to the table. "You know he's still missing."

Edna fell against the refrigerator and shook her head. Neecey watched Edna's face. There was annoyance in the shift of Edna's eyes, in the twist of her lips. Ruby always wanted to talk about Jerome, like Edna wasn't almost twenty-six with a boutique opening soon and more men trailing behind her than drummers behind a majorette. Even Neecey could tell that she was a canyon filled with new dreams.

"We're divorced, Ruby," Edna replied. "I don't know why you worry about Jerome. Didn't he almost kill Neecey?"

"Wasn't like that, Edna," Neecey said as she rolled the coffee cup between her hands.

The doorbell rang and Ruby yelled, "Jack, if that's another one of yo' friends at the door, I'm kicking you out."

She placed a platter of golden brown catfish in the center of the table between the spaghetti and garlic bread. The steam from the spaghetti sauce wafted into the light above the table. The scent of oregano, basil, and garlic teased Neecey's appetite. Neecey lifted a crispy piece of fish from the platter and plopped into the chair at the head of the table.

"Odessa, hand me a napkin," she said as she peeled a hunk of meat from the tail.

"You should wait," Odessa said. "We're eating as soon as Edna gets the china and silver."

"China and silver," Edna mimicked. "White girl, you mean the plates and forks."

"Neecey, Ruby," Jack called from the living room. "Come to the door."

"What for?" Ruby asked.

"We're not buying anything, Jack," Neecey said.

"There's a man asking for you and Ruby. He says his name is Jesse." Jack's voice was tight and angry.

Neecey dropped the piece of fish on the table and rose. She and Ruby moved like zombies past Edna. Odessa never moved from the kitchen table, never stopped tearing the lettuce into shreds. In the living room, Jesse stood on the other side of the latched screen door, looking ancient with wrinkles crisscrossing his face. His body was lost in oversized clothing. He removed a stained brown hat from his head. His hair was gray and his caramel eyes were dull. Serenda walked up to Neecey and laid her head on her shoulder. For a moment, Neecey wanted to stroke her brow, to soothe her, to say, "It's okay, baby. Daddy's home."

Ruby spoke first. "Jesse?"

"Yeah, it's me," he said and looked first at Neecey, then at Jack still holding the door, poised to slam it on a moment's notice.

"Look at y'all," he said. "All grown and fine looking."

"Daddy?" Neecey said. He looked into her eyes and smiled, that slow lazy Jesse smile. His dull eyes filled with tears that added some of the sparkle Neecey remembered. *Got women around my door like hounds,* she heard Ruby say from the past.

"Yeah, sweetie," Jesse said and Neecey pushed past Jack and opened the screen door. She leaped into Jesse's arms, and he tried to balance himself. She wrapped her arms around his neck and wept.

"Y'all come on in this house," Ruby said. "Folks talk about us enough without y'all huddled on my front stoop. Come on, Jesse, I got a fresh pot of coffee on."

"I just wanted to see my kids," he said. "I don't want to disturb y'all."

"Man, get yo' ass in this house," Ruby said with a laugh. It was reminiscent of a past voice, before Manny, Earl, David, and before all the children. Neecey clasped Jesse's hand. His fingers, large and rough, were much bigger than she remembered. He closed his hands around her fingers and followed her into the house.

The family was silent. They watched Neecey and Ruby escort the man through the house. There was tightness in Jack's face and a condescending sneer on Odessa's face. Only Edna, Serenda, Jordan, and Darcy looked on with puzzlement. They had no claim to the man, knew of him only because Neecey, Jack, and Odessa had shared memories of him.

"Come on in the kitchen," Ruby said.

"Still making the kitchen the main room, I see," Jesse said.

"Once a mule gets set in her ways . . ." Ruby began.

"All she does is age," Jesse said, finishing the old joke between them. "Oh, y'all was getting ready for dinner."

"Man, sit down," Ruby said. "You're welcome to join us."

"Crap!" Jack said from the doorway.

"Where have you been?" Neecey asked without preliminaries. "What happened to you?"

Jesse gave Ruby a quizzical look. She simply shook her head. "I didn't tell them. I didn't tell them."

"Tell us what?" Jack shouted. "Tell us what a no-good bum he is."

"Jack!" Neecey exclaimed.

"Well, he just walked out on us and now he wanna walk back in, with a 'Hi, I'm Jesse.'"

"Boy," Ruby warned.

"He's . . ."

"Jack, that's enough," Neecey warned. "He's still family."

"That's stretching it, Neecey," Jack said. "Even for you. And ask him where has he been for almost fourteen years. Ask him that."

No one spoke as Jesse slipped into the chair Neecey held for him. He placed his hat on his knee. He looked around at Odessa, who now sat at the head of the table slicing red tomatoes. She looked at him with disdainful eyes and puckered lips. He recognized Della in that look. He looked at Serenda, leaning against Neecey. He looked at the angry young man standing between him and Ruby, daring him to reclaim her, reclaim him, reclaim any part of this life, and finally, he looked into Neecey's eyes, hazel eyes, questioning him, begging him, for what?

"I've been in prison," he whispered.

NEECEY SAT IN THE PASSENGER'S SEAT and watched the South Side landscape of Lake Shore Drive fly past in splendid summer green and, although she would soon shake her head at the filthiness of Lake Michigan, this day it was a deep sapphire blue. In the distance the flat black top of McCormick Place loomed. *Fourteen years,* she thought as she watched Jesse's swollen fingers steady the steering wheel. *Ruby never said a word. Della, Pete, and Ma'Dear never breathed the secret.* Her jaws tightened and she bit her lower lip.

"What's wrong?" Jesse asked as he took a quick glance at her.

She shook her head, "Nothing, I'm thinking about Mc-Cormick Place. That's all."

"Yeah, they did a good job," he said. "I read it can hold three times more exhibits than before. Chicago has changed so much since I've been gone. That Dan Ryan el, whew! I rode it. Coming around Twenty-second Street, I thought I would plummet to my death. And the Sears Tower, man oh man, how long did it take to build that thing?"

Neecey smiled and said nothing but snuggled into the seat. She could hear Ruby snap whenever they asked about their daddy. *Daddy? What daddy? You see a daddy around here?* Neecey wiped her brow again. How could she sweat with the wind whipping across her face? How could all the grown-ups, even Della, lie to them? How could they pretend that he just walked off the earth? And why had they—she, Jack, and Odessa—stopped asking about him, pushed him far, far away in a memory crypt?

The car—an old something, she didn't know, didn't care—was black with leather seats and in its day it may have been a beauty. Now it was just a big old car that smelled of cigarettes and booze and funk. They flew past the aquarium and Jesse's voice changed, grew deep and serious.

"Young and thought I knew everything," he said. "Ruby was right. I was whorish. The women loved me and I was whorish. She said 'Jesse, you can't have both of us—either Gwen or me.' And Gwen, well, she had stuff on me. Knew stuff I couldn't share with Ruby. Like my business. I couldn't afford to piss her off. She threatened to drop a dime on me if I didn't leave Ruby. What difference did it make? I left Ruby and ended up in jail anyway. Ten years for transporting over state lines in a pickup truck and fifteen years for assault with a weapon. Stupid."

He turned onto Balboa and drove over to State Street. The Pacific Garden Mission, peep shows, adult bookstores, and taverns lined the small strip from Harrison to Van Buren. In the heart of the loop, at Madison, he headed west. Soon the loop was behind them. They crossed over the expressway, past Halsted and into a stretch of tenements and taverns. Tattered curtains and window shades fluttered in the breeze.

"Look out there," Jesse said. "What do you see?"

Winos and prostitutes strolled across Madison, the city's skid row. Their bodies and their clothes were filthy. Urine and funk permeated the air. Neecey didn't want to tell him she saw bums. She didn't want to hurt him because he looked like those bums, worn, depressed, with misery on his face like pancake makeup.

"Bums," she said quietly.

"That's what everybody sees." He smirked and shook his head. "I see men with names nobody remembers. I see women so low they can't recall their mamas' faces. Look, see that man?" He lifted one finger and subtly pointed ahead to a guy in a screaming lime-green silk shirt and tight black pants. The guy stood on the corner nonchalantly as if he was waiting for a bus. "He's a pusher," Jesse said, "just selling these grown kids the candy they crave. That's what I did before I went to jail."

Jesse waited for a reaction from Neecey. Neecey watched the man as the car rolled passed him. The man nodded at her and she quickly turned her head.

"I was strung out when they arrested me. Thought I was being cool. Thought I could handle it, but in jail I found out that dope had handled me. And even when I hit that concrete floor, there was nobody to help me up. I was alone and Gwen didn't post bail, didn't hire a lawyer, and took all the money I had stashed with her and bought a house and a husband and left me in jail to rot. And Ma'Dear didn't answer my letters, didn't hire a lawyer, acted like I wasn't her son. Pete and Ruby just disappeared from my life. I got divorce papers through the mail, but no birthday card and no visits. A thousand nights passed before the pain went away. If I had murdered somebody, I think they would have come and protested my innocence, but during my trial, only one face stood by me. Della's. And in jail, I was alone. All I wanted to do, sweetie, was to make enough money like Pete to buy Ruby a house. I think Della understood that. She was my only visitor up until she died. She sent me pictures of y'all. Those pictures kept me going for a long time."

They rode farther west through the decaying West Side. The aftermath of the 1968 riots was still evident in the burned buildings and demolished businesses. It would take the West Side over thirty years to recover. As they drove through the neighborhood, Jesse pointed out pushers, and suppliers, and children who were also dope addicts.

"I'm showing you all this," he said, "'cause I want you to know the world has many faces, Neecey. What you see on the surface is not always the true story. What you hear is not always the truth."

"The worst thing 'bout being locked away is daydreaming. I useta dream about y'all. Some nights I could hear you and Jack in my cell arguing, sometimes I could see you and Odessa playing on the floor before my eyes, and then a cellmate would walk across that space and y'all would disappear and I knew there was no hope. I was alone. I learned not to daydream about y'all. I would think about something stupid, like how many jelly beans could you fit in a shoe.

"I didn't expect none of y'all to welcome me." He looked at

her and smiled. "I can't blame Jack for calling me a jailbird. I can't blame Odessa for not wanting anything to do with me. Poor Serenda was just a baby. None of y'all knows me, but you're still my Neecey. You always did see good even when there was none."

Jesse fell quiet and maneuvered the car along the Dan Ryan Expressway. He exited at Seventy-first Street and sped toward Ruby's house. Neecey wanted to open her mouth and speak, to tell him that the years had not been good for her either. She ached to tell him about Manny and how she had to watch over the girls, but the years had erased the freedom she once had with him. He was a stranger, an adulterer, a dope pusher, and a jailbird. He was her father, her daddy. He was all of that and none of that. She watched all that was familiar fly past her window: Hi-Low Foods, White's Shrimp, the currency exchange, the cemetery, the corner tavern, the hot dog stand, and finally Ruby's zinnias bordering the walkway. She could not get the words out to tell him that her life had been an untended weed patch.

"You know Ma'Dear and Pete told me a lot about what's been going on," Jesse said as he stopped in front of the house. "The last two weeks since I've been home, all Ma'Dear can talk about is what Ruby has put all y'all through. When I see the control you have over Jack and Ruby and everybody else in that house, I know you didn't have it easy. No, that kind of respect and power don't come easy."

He turned and looked at her. He smiled. He touched her face. His fingers slid down to her chin and he gripped it gently. In that touch, she felt finality, a finishing.

"Sweetie, you're stronger than the lot of them," Jesse said. "If I could make up for all those years, I would. But they're gone. Wasted and burned. Let me give you one piece of advice—sometimes in order to save others, you have to save yourself first."

Neecey wanted to tell him exactly what she had been through. She wanted him to know what he and Ruby had done to her, how they left her to fight off Booker and Keith. She wanted to know why he never wrote to her. She would have answered his letters . . .

Dear Daddy, she would have written. *We miss you. Please hurry home and save us before Ruby kills us. Love, Neecey.*

As he drove away, Neecey watched the sun set over the cemetery. A shiver ran up her spine. In six months, he would die in Ma'Dear's basement, a needle stuck in his arm like an arrow. She turned and walked toward the house. As she reached the door, Jack flung it open.

"He's gone?" he asked.

She heard Jesse's voice from a long time ago, when she asked if the bogeyman was gone. "Yes, sweetie. He's gone."

chapter 17

SONG OF THE JEWELED BIRD

*t*HE BIRD WAS EXOTIC, with bright turquoise and fiery coral feathers. She had the face of a parakeet, small, delicate, with tiny eyes, but the large prominent body of a toucan. She was a combination of South American birds that Neecey had seen in *National Geographic*. She squawked and flew madly around the room, knocking small crystal figurines off of a wall shelf, fluttering against Manny's waterfall mural with the half-naked nymphs, leaving droppings on the furniture. The bird careened and flew into the plate-glass window. There was no way out. The bird flew into Neecey's face and squawked. The large bullhorn sound stirred Neecey's Afro. The bird squawked again and Neecey jumped. Her eyes were no longer tiny parakeet eyes, nor were they the baleful eyes of a toucan. Neecey's own hazel eyes stared back at her. The bird rose above her head. She fluttered around and around. Her wings grew and expanded until they touched the opposing walls of the large room. Her toucan body sagged under the weight of those wings.

"There's no way out," Neecey cried. "The windows are sealed."

The bird squawked and rose until its back pressed against the ceiling. Jewel-colored feathers floated down, fluffy and colorful, but when they hit the floor they were spiny and bare. The translucent spine glimmered and then dissipated into ash. More and more feathers fell and ashes rose around her stacked heels, around the hem of her elephant-leg pants. The feathers on the bird's wings were thick and lustrous, but its body was as bald as a plucked chicken. Yellow fat oozed from its pores. The fat fell like large raindrops and mingled with the dust around her feet. The mire rose up to the calves of her legs. The bird squawked and arched its back. Whack, whack, whack. It knocked against the ceiling. Plaster, round and crumbly as pie dough, fell and rolled off the bird's back. Whack! Whack! Whack! Squaaawk, squaaawk, squaaawk. The sounds twirled around her. A shimmer of light filtered through a pinhole in the ceiling. The light revolved like a searchlight as the opening grew bigger and bigger until Neecey could see the moon and sun in a cobalt sky.

"Yes," she cried. "We are east of the sun and west of the moon."

Whack! Whack! Whack! The ceiling disappeared. The featherless bird swooped and picked Neecey up in its claws and rose, rose, rose from the room. High in the sky, Neecey looked down. Now, she saw that the room was only a tiny closet filled with family.

"Good-bye," she cried and with those words the bird opened its claws and Neecey fell, back, back, back through the dark-light sky, back.

"If only I had wings," she cried. "If only . . ."

The bird soared high above the house, spread its wings, and flew away, away—moving beyond the sights and sounds of the family, moving away from the pull of the house. In Neecey's dream, she cried, "If only I had wings. If only."

THE IF ONLY OF NEECEY'S DREAM manifested in the spring of 1973, when Manny's eighteen-wheeler jackknifed, rammed into another eighteen-wheeler, skittered into five cars, and finally rested in a small ravine on I-65, just north of the exit to Lafayette, Indiana. It was considered one of the worst highway accidents in northern Indiana history: eight people were killed, three were traumatically injured, one person slipped into a coma and remained there for two years before death claimed her, and Manny was airlifted to the best trauma unit in the Midwest—Cook County Hospital. The doctors wired and set, stitched, and pasted Manny back together the best way they could. Yet, all the wiring and stitching could not make Manny whole. He was pronounced paralyzed from the neck down.

The first time Neecey stepped into the hospital room with Ruby, she pressed her fist to her mouth and groaned. Tubes twisted around Manny like a mass of snakes: in his arms, up his nose, in his mouth, and snaking from under the sheets into a plastic pouch. A steel bar arched from one side of his head to the other and was bolted, yes bolted, into his scalp. A long thin wire ran from the steel bar over the edge of the bed to sandbags on the floor. This, Neecey later learned, was to keep his neck and head perfectly still. The wire, the tubes, the oxygen tanks, the monitor, the deep hum of the machinery, and Manny's breathing heightened the massive horror of his face. His nose was swollen and black stitches ran along one side. His purple lips were opened to reveal pointy and shattered teeth. A continuous stream of red saliva ran through the tube hooked over his mouth. His usually fat and puffy jaws were sunken, ashen. Blood and mucus encrusted his head and face, although Neecey could see parts of his neck and face had been cleaned. Neecey walked around the bed, eyeing Manny from different angles, looking for the big burly guy, the familiar in this strange convoluted face. In this bed, Manny was helpless, small, dying.

Ruby sat in the chair next to the bed. Her pocketbook fell to the floor with a thud. She flopped back in the chair and sobbed, "What am I gonna do?"

The mother, small and crumpled in her blue plaid coat, and the daughter, stern and upright, stared at each other. Ruby looked around the room at the bed table shoved against the far wall and the drab drapes on the suspension wire. She stared at the oxygen tank and the black bag that pulsated as Manny sucked air.

"Oh, Lord," Ruby cried and dropped her head into her hands. "What am I gonna do?"

"Get a hold of yourself, Ruby," Neecey said. "You can't sit in here weeping. What if he wakes up? You want him to think he's dying?"

"Better if he had," Ruby snapped.

"Ruby!"

"I can't sit here," Ruby cried. She leaped out of the chair, kicking her pocketbook over and bolted for the door. "I can't stand hospitals." Ruby brushed passed the nurse who entered with a fresh IV bag. The nurse leaped out of Ruby's way. Neecey watched the tail end of the blue plaid coat disappear.

"Are you his daughter?" the nurse asked as she moved to the head of Manny's bed. She took the used bag off the IV stand.

Manny's daughter? Neecey thought.

"Stepdaughter," she said. "I'm his stepdaughter."

She was the stepdaughter who sat in the cinders and watched the ogre terrorize the mother. She was the stepdaughter who spun the straw into gold to supplement the money the ogre threw at the mother. She was the stepdaughter who now watched his body degenerate into her freedom. She thought, *Now I can move,* and the moment she thought it, such overwhelming guilt smothered her that she again put her fist to her mouth, sucked in air, and groaned. Tears flowed down her face. Neecey looked down at the crumpled man. She wanted to move, to be free, but she had never wished him mangled, dead. Had she?

"Oh, you must be close," the nurse said. She walked over to Neecey and embraced her. "He's getting the best care. The doctors are doing everything."

The nurse's cologne, inexpensive Heaven's Scent from Walgreen's drugstore, could not mask the cigarette odor that clung to her hair and clothes, nor the smell of death-decaying bodies nor the medicinal stench that held the room, the floor, and the hospital in its grip.

Neecey pulled away from the nurse. She wondered what indeed would be the best care for Manny—to pull all the tubes out of his body, to let him rot in his own blood, or to add one more stitch to his mangled body? What would be the best care for them all? Manny was, and had been, a thorn. But she had never wished him dead. Had she?

She tried to remember one good Manny moment. After ten years, there had to be one good moment that they shared. She thought about holidays and birthdays and other special occasions, and she saw what she never wanted to see—Manny with presents, grumpy ideas for Christmas, the Fourth of

July—"Ruby, just pack a damn picnic and let's go to Brookfield Zoo. Too hot in this apartment for fifty people to be crowded under each other."

And that had been the way of all his outings, his suggestions, given almost begrudgingly. Money spent begrudgingly. Here gal, go get some Popsicles for y'all. Maybe that'll keep y'all mouths closed. Everything harsh and mean. Everything. She saw it all. Him. Him. Him. Throwing money at them like they were street urchins. Go get some damn shoes for Jordan before her toes hit the ground. Never a nice word, but always, always on time. Perfect timing.

When she looked down at him, at the nurse switching the intravenous bag, she saw the predator in him, that beast with claws that haunted her dreams. That thing waiting in dark corners and hallways, the wicked man in him that could not, would not, be tamed. She knew what was in her heart was true. He would have touched them.

ALWAYS RUBY'S LONG, manicured fingers tapped impatiently against her purse, waiting to flee the hospital, the stench of disinfectant, the drone of machinery, the starched white of uniforms, the drab greens, gurneys, trays, IVs, and the always present nurse's button—to escape her broken-up husband. Neecey simply waited for Manny to stabilize. Once conscious and stable, Manny watched Neecey with a foreboding despair. For weeks, he could make only guzzling sounds. His teeth were splintered and his tongue lacerated and swollen. He ignored Ruby's presence in his hospital room. Yet, there was a constant silent plea as his eyes followed Neecey.

Manny, sensing desperation in Ruby by the way she never really looked at him, or touched him, or cried, or screamed, or raged at the misfortune that had befallen her husband, sensing that Ruby was counting up the dollars his accident would bring her, sensing that she would be no comfort, no joy, and no friend to him, searched Neecey's eyes. Neecey would know what to do. Still, she spoke no reassuring words, no promises.

Ruby hired a lawyer and filed for power of attorney and guardianship over her incapacitated husband, and then, before Manny got the use of his tongue, she filed a lawsuit against the trucking company. By the time Manny had the use of his voice and was nearing release from the hospital, Ruby was his legal legs, eyes, and voice. Visiting Manny in the hospital became a regular thing to do for Neecey, like a notation on a pad: pick up dry cleaning, make appointment for dentist, visit Manny, stop at Walgreen's. She would have stopped the visits if Ruby had been diligent in her own visits. Ruby, who never took to sickness, visited only enough to keep the hospital staff from calling her a bad wife.

The day Neecey signed the lease for the studio apartment on Pine Grove and Addison, she walked into Manny's room, expecting to find him flat on his back, but the bolts, rod, and sandbag were gone and Manny was propped up in bed with pillows.

"Where's Ruby?" he asked. His voice was still thick and slurry from months of disuse. His long and thin arms lay useless on the sheet.

"I don't know," she said and placed her knapsack on the chair beside his bed and looked at him. "How are you today?"

She noticed that his arms and fingers had lost their beefiness. After three months in the hospital, loose skin covered his bones. She moved to the end of his bed and looked directly in his face. His nose and lips were normal size again, but both had telltale signs of trauma: scars and ridges. His eyes, sunken like gullies in his wide face, looked up at her. The bar and bolts had been gone for three weeks, but still the indentations and bald spots remained. She knew that hair would never again grow in those spots.

It was always difficult talking to him. He had no interests other than his mangled rig and his pension. Yes, it was true, she told him again and again, there was no way he could have stopped on that rainy highway. The brake lines were faulty. And yes, Ruby is paying all the bills.

"Could you open those curtains?" he asked.

She walked to the window and pulled the drawstrings. Sunlight, bright afternoon sunlight, flooded the room. Out of the window, she could see people flocking into the main entrance. She saw others walking across the green commons to the Congress–Jefferson Park el. The things that you took for granted, she thought. She could run out of the building, across that green expanse to the el, north to her new apartment, south to Manny's home, anywhere she pleased, but he couldn't. He could not do anything but wait for others to help him. When she turned from the window, he was staring at her.

"You grew up to be a nice-looking woman," he said slowly. "I thought you were gonna be a fat thing. If it wasn't for those eyes popping out yo' head, you would be beautiful."

"Like I care what you think," she snapped.

"No sense in getting nippy," he said.

His eyes and brow squinted, making a deep V in the center of his head. He watched her tighten her wide mouth until her lips disappeared. While he was flat on his back, she looked taller than five feet four inches. She slowly walked from the window to the edge of his bed. Her bulging eyes never left his face. Her lips sneered and turned down, while her nose squinted up.

"I'm moving," she said.

"Moving?" The frown left his face. His face was blank, empty of emotion.

"Yeah, you finally getting rid of me," she said and sat in the second chair. "I found a studio apartment, up north, far, far away from your house."

"Why now?" he asked.

She said nothing.

"Are you happy?"

"Happy?" Neecey asked as she scooted back in the chair.

"About me?"

"About you?"

"I can't move. I'm not whole."

"Manny, you were never whole," she said and tucked her legs under the chair.

His face contorted. She said nothing. The rumbling of the dinner cart came through the open doorway, along with the moans of other patients, the cries of some family, and the footsteps of staff rushing back and forth. In Manny's room, their breathing filled the space. Neecey looked at him, sitting like a statue with only his head moving from her, to the window, to the door, and back to her.

"You picked a bad time to be moving."

"Bad for whom?" she asked.

He said nothing. He thought of Ruby, running through his savings, his small pension, and whatever money she would get from the trucking company. He thought of the months and years he would lie in the bedroom, where Ruby would put him and forget about him. Wasn't she always talking about Vegas, Hollywood, always talking about the show business career she could have had. Ruby would leave him in the dark room calling for her—for someone to help him.

"We need you," he said flatly. His eyes pleaded, "Forgive me, Neecey, for I have sinned."

"I'm moving," she said and turned her head. She did not want to cave in to his soft, pleading eyes. She would not let him make her forget the years of watching and guarding, of playing soldier.

"Neecey," he called.

She turned back to him. He looked into her eyes and saw the thirteen-year-old girl who stood him down with nothing more than a thunderous look in her eyes. He looked and saw the fifteen-year-old girl who commanded an army of children against him; he looked at the woman before him, svelte and composed. Her hazel eyes were wide and fringed with long but sparse eyelashes. There was a hardness in her eyes whenever she visited him, but he had seen the softness there; when she talked to her sisters and brother her face relaxed and her eyes smiled.

"Who hurt you, Neecey?" he asked.

"What?" she asked. Her brow wrinkled into a frown and her jaw tightened. His question traveled down into her heart, past the years, past the place where she knew all the answers, past the empty places, into the dark, slimy hole that was her youth, where she had bottled up the bogeyman, Booker, Keith, extension cords, red screams, red, red, red screams.

"Somebody hurt you."

"You don't know what you're talking about!" she snapped.

"Somebody hurt you and you want to punish me," he said. "You've always wanted to hurt me, kill me."

"You listen. Ever since I was a little girl, I've known men like you."

"Not me."

"Like you."

"I've never done anything to you."

"'Cause I never let you."

"You hate me that much?"

"I've never hated you, Manny," she said. "But I've never trusted you."

"You won't help me."

She looked at the liquid swimming in his eyes. His soulful expression. He was frightened, but there was nothing she could do. She had wings, beautiful jewel-colored wings, and she would use them, yes, she would and fly . . . fly . . . east of the sun, west of the moon.

chapter 18

THE SORRY SONG

*N*EECEY'S PHONE SHRILLED as she entered her studio apartment. She dumped her bags on the table next to the door and dashed for the phone. Once again she hoped it was not a complaint call from Ruby about the plight of her life. *Manny is too much. The girls won't listen to me. I can't be tied down.* Ruby tried to use Manny and the girls to drag her back into that heavy world. Neecey dreaded the phone calls as they cut into her freedom.

Yet, Neecey was free. She was free to fill her apartment with the scent of Chanel No. 19, Pine Sol disinfectant cleaner, or burnt toast. She was free to step out of the shower and let the water drip from her bronze body as she walked from room to room. She was free to sit in the middle of her sofa bed with a large mixing bowl of crunchy cereal; free to leave a permanent spoon in the New York cherry ice cream. For once, she was not mother, protector, provider. For once, she did not have to think about consequences, results, possibilities, probabilities, or responsibilities. *Let it be one of the girls,* she thought as she picked up the phone.

"Neecey?" Ruby spoke first.

"Hello, Ruby," Neecey said dryly and searched for a Hershey's Kiss in a candy dish.

"Girl, where have you been?" Ruby asked. "I've been calling you all day."

"Yeah?" Neecey mumbled into the phone. She plopped on the sofa and closed her eyes. Ruby's voice interfered with the tranquillity of her studio. Her beige sofa and three pale bookcases were the only furniture. She had no chairs, no kitchen table. All her meals were eaten on the sofa.

"Chauncey's body is being shipped home!" Ruby said without preliminaries.

"Chauncey's what?" Neecey asked.

"The Vietnamese government released more bodies. His is one of them."

"No," Neecey said and leaned forward. Her desire for chocolate disappeared. She knew nothing about this brother. Nothing. He was a name, Chauncey. She had no vision of him. The one picture Edna had of Chauncey was old and faded, from another time. He had been missing for so long.

Ruby was saying, "The body will be in Mississippi on Tuesday and the services will be on Wednesday. I thought you should know."

Neecey was old enough to listen to death's soft footsteps and not tremble with fear. She was old enough to stand beside a coffin, to feel the paleness of death, to hear death's hollow laughter in the chambers of her heart. And there were chambers filled with memories of Della, Eddie, Jesse, and now Chauncey. Chambers that should have been filled with hope and dreams, chambers where flames yet burned, life yet burned.

She had borne Della's death because there were many Della-memories to fill those Della-chambers. And Neecey had borne the horror of Eddie's death with Jerome and Edna, held on to the memory of a playful baby who looked more like Edna than any of the siblings. Neecey had held Edna's hands through the services, stood by her side at the grave, loved her out of that sorrow, and hummed, just like Della.

And alone she had borne the arrows of Jesse's death. Ma'Dear and Ruby wailed and cried. Uncle Pete sat like a mute with his eyes focused on the cross above the pulpit. Tears ran down Serenda's face like soft showers. Odessa, composed and dignified, dabbed at her eyes with her lace handkerchief. Jack had been conspicuously absent. Yet, she alone remembered the rage in Jesse's soul, knew that death had met him—alone.

Neecey didn't have a memory to fill Chauncey's chamber. Death had borne him home long ago, this she knew. Now, infinite mercy provided an opportunity for her to say good-bye to a brother she never touched, a brother who rested from war. She would go. She would say hello and good-bye. She would be a part of his life for a few minutes, a few hours. She would share the perfumey flowers and the grief-invoking hymns. Yes, she would eat the respite afterward, for it would be the last and only supper she would share with this brother.

"Aren't you going?" she asked Ruby.

"Naw," Ruby said. "Who's going to keep Manny?"

"Ruby, he was your son!" Neecey exclaimed. "You could hire somebody to take care of Manny."

"I'm not paying good money for somebody to watch a cripple," Ruby said.

"You need to go, Ruby," Neecey said. "I'll call Edna and see when she's leaving . . ."

"She's already gone."

"You're really not going?"

"No."

THE MOMENT NEECEY opened the door of Ruby's house, she knew something was wrong. The drapes at the window were drawn and the house was still, like the stillness of a mortuary. She kicked the door closed and the house was swallowed by darkness. She stood for a moment and listened for a sound of life—a cough, a fart, a sigh—as Ruby's house was never empty. She heard a steady whimpering in the kitchen. She listened. The sound looped around the room, past the curio cabinet filled with glass figurines, the silent piano, the orange floral sofa, around the room in a circle, behind the drapes, the console stereo, and the matching armchair next to the walk-in closet. The sound looped around the room and hooked Neecey. She took small baby steps as if she were playing a game of Captain, May I. Just inside the kitchen, she gasped. Darcy huddled in the corner next to the dining table. Her knees were drawn up her to chin and her blood-spotted housecoat was stretched down to her feet. Thick, bloody welts covered her arms, which were wrapped around most of her body. Her Afro was more than uncombed—it was twisted into clumps.

"Oh Laud, Darcy!" Neecey cried.

Darcy leaped up from the corner and pushed aside the chair that stood between her and Neecey. She threw her arms around Neecey's neck and sobbed, "I hate her! I hate her!"

"Who, Darcy?" Neecey asked, knowing as she asked that these welts were the results of Ruby and her extension cord.

"Ruby," Darcy screamed. "I hate her!"

"Don't say that, Darcy!" Neecey exclaimed.

"She hates me and I hate her! You think I don't know she thinks of me as poison? Bane. What kinda name is Bane? She's not my mother. She's not."

"Why did she do this?" Neecey asked, touching one of the welts. She knew that welt was much too deep and when it healed a shiny brown keloid would remain, like the one on her own leg.

"'Cause I won't bathe Manny."

"What?" Neecey asked. Her voice was tiny, so tiny.

"She tried to kill me because I won't bathe him."

"Where's Ruby?" Neecey asked. "And Serenda and Jordan?"

"Ruby went next door, and Serenda took a job at McDonald's." Darcy pulled away from her. She took a wad of tissue out of her pocket and blew her nose. "Jordan's doing it," Darcy whispered.

Neecey's head throbbed. She leaned against the wall. She was ten again and everything was wrong. Neecey could do nothing but sit and let the grown-ups have their way with her, toss her around like a beanbag, hurt her, hurt her so bad that it was all dark and lonely inside. Hurt her so bad that all she heard in her head was her own sorry song. A hum. A long hum that had to end.

"What did you say?" she asked Darcy.

"Jordan's upstairs doing it."

"Oh, Laud!" Neecey pushed Darcy aside and rushed across the kitchen. She took the stairs two at a time. "Jordan! Stop! Stop, Jordan!"

"I told her not to do it," Darcy said as she followed Neecey up the stairs. "But you know how scared Jordan is of a whupping."

The short hall had four doors opening into three bedrooms and a bathroom. Neecey could feel it growing, stretching—the master bedroom moving farther and farther away from her. She could not reach the doorknob quickly enough.

"Who closed the door?" Neecey bellowed.

"Ruby," Darcy stated.

Neecey burst through the door in time to see Jordan, her face red and sweating, struggling to turn Manny on his side. He wore only a pair of boxer shorts. Her small green eyes were puffy from crying. A washbasin sat on the dresser next to the four-poster bed. Water had sloshed out of the basin onto the dresser, the floor, and the bed. Manny's skin glistened with water.

"Neecey, he's too heavy for me," Jordan cried.

"Drop him," Neecey calmly said. Yes, that was her voice. Cold, cold as the hawk off Lake Michigan. Cold as Capone. Cold as all the dead hope in her heart.

"What?" Jordan asked.

"I said drop him."

Jordan released Manny and he flopped onto his back. Jordan looked from Darcy in the doorway to Neecey. Neecey's face was dark, darker than her usual brown color, dark and ugly, like a rubber Halloween mask, all scrunched.

"Ruby told me to," Jordan explained.

"Get out of here!" Neecey said. "Both of you."

Jordan tried to ease around Neecey, but Neecey grabbed her arm. "Don't you ever, ever touch him again. He's a dangerous man."

"He can't move."

"His tongue isn't paralyzed," Neecey said.

Jordan dropped her head and Neecey knew, knew that Manny had gotten to her. She wheeled around and saw the smirk on Manny's face. His round head, propped up on the pillows, shone like polished brass.

"Manny!" she shouted. "You pervert! What did you say to her?"

"Nothing," Manny said and lowered his eyes.

"You lie," she said and stormed up to the bed. She looked down at him and did not see fear or remorse, but a smug *you can't do anything about it* look.

"What did he say to you, Jordan?" Neecey asked in a low voice.

"He didn't say anything . . ."

Neecey jerked her head around, arched one eyebrow, and looked at Jordan. Jordan's yellow skin flushed to a berry red. Under that stare, Jordan shivered and wiped her hands on her jeans. Behind her, Darcy glared at Manny, who still wore a smirk.

"What did he say?" Neecey enunciated the words slowly.

The room tightened in her anger. The tall, dark armoire, with its intricate design of leaves, smothered the wall next to the door. The dark green draperies at the window blocked most of the sunlight. The room was filled with all their breathing, Manny's raspy breath on the bed, Jordan's steady breath, Darcy's deep puffs of anger, and Neecey's controlled breathing.

"What did he say?" Neecey repeated.

Nervously, Jordan wiped her hands on her bell-bottoms and whispered, "He kept calling me *pretty thang*. Kept saying how good my hands felt."

The front door slammed. Ruby's footsteps resounded through the house. Darcy walked into the room and stood beside Neecey. Jordan moved over to the armoire and positioned her back against it. Manny looked at Neecey with hooded eyes and a small tight smirk. Rage, deep-seated rage boiled and rose slowly like lava from the bowl of her stomach. She heard the cries from a thousand beatings. All the hurt, the unhealed hurt in her heart swelled. She felt, once again, all the licks from Ruby's extension cord cutting into her skin. Neecey was ten years old with a knife in her hand, and there was nothing she could do but feel the licks and feel the terror.

"Damn you, Ruby!" Neecey cried and rushed to the dresser. She lifted the washbasin and slung it across the bed. The water arced and splashed on her, on Manny, and on the bed while the basin hit the closed window. The glass shattered and, instinctively, Manny closed his eyes. Jordan screamed.

"What the hell is going on up there?" Ruby shouted.

Neecey, with one swoop of her hand, sent Ruby's collection of perfume atomizers and makeup into a liquid mess between the bed and dresser. With no thought to herself, to her hand, she slammed the mirror above the dresser. The mirror shattered. She hit the mirror repeatedly.

"Neecey, Neecey," Darcy cried. She wrapped her arms around Neecey and pulled her away from the mirror.

"My mirror!" Ruby screamed from the doorway.

Neecey and Darcy saw the shattered image of Ruby in the mirror. Manny looked at Neecey, then at Ruby. Neecey turned slowly around, pulling Darcy with her. Neecey snatched herself from Darcy's arms.

"You tell me, Ruby," she hissed. "Tell me. Why is Jordan up here bathing your husband?"

"Girl, you ain't got no say about what goes on in here," Manny instigated.

"Shut up, Manny, before I smother you," Neecey said as she whirled around toward him. "You should have died. You are a sick pervert. You can't feel a thing, but here you are saying stuff like that to a girl you supposedly raised like a daughter. You should have died, Manny."

Manny clamped his mouth shut and looked at Ruby for help. Ruby's eyes went from the broken mirror to the shattered window and all the details in between: the broken bottles of perfume between the dresser and the bed, the water-drenched bed, Jordan's scared face, Manny's smirk, Darcy's sneer, and Neecey's rage. Neecey kicked a broken crystal atomizer.

"You are destroying your daughters, Ruby. Darcy and Jordan are young girls. They have no business bathing your paralyzed husband. What's wrong with you? Are you so shallow, so stingy, and so hateful that you can have little girls bathe your man? From this moment on, they do not touch him. Do you understand me?"

"Who do you think you talking to, girl?" Ruby asked with bravado. "Get out my house. Get the hell out of my house, before I call the police!"

"You call them, Ruby! You call them and explain why your fifteen-year-old daughter is bathing your naked husband. Then you explain why your sixteen-year-old girl is bleeding across the back and neck from an extension cord."

"I want you out of here," Ruby said. "And don't come back!"

Neecey slumped against Darcy. She saw clearly for the first time that Ruby's children were outcasts in her heart. Rejects. Neecey's throat was on fire and the ache in her ear had grown. She was in a dark place, a dark, dark place, and Ruby stood before her, trying to gather strength, trying to conjure up something that would subvert Neecey back into a docile creature. There was a gathering in Neecey's soul, in her heart. There was a surge of dreams and a loosening of so much pain, so much hurt. This woman was simply someone who had birthed her and forgotten her in the same moment. This woman loved only the image in her mirror.

"As long as Serenda, Darcy, and Jordan are under this roof, I'll be here," Neecey said, pointing to the floor.

"Who the hell do you think you are?" Ruby asked. "Who the hell . . ."

"She's our mother," Darcy interrupted from behind Neecey. "She's always been our mother."

A sob caught in Neecey's throat. She looked at Darcy, who nodded her assurance. Jordan joined them and wrapped her arms around Neecey. Ruby gasped. Her hand covered her heart and clenched and unclenched. She was confronted by women she could not recognize. They stood united before her, like they had as children.

"Told you to put her out a long time ago," Manny said.

"Shut up, Manny," Ruby said.

"No more, Ruby," Neecey said and led the girls to the door. "No more."

Neecey rode home on the North-South el. She huddled against the train and pressed her forehead against the window. How did Ruby define love? Yes, Neecey could point to moments of fun, moments of peace, moments of serenity, but she could not point to moments where Ruby's love for her children was evident. She could not recall ever hearing Ruby say "I love you" to any one of the children dangling around the hem of her skirt. There had been tears and rage, but no love. Neecey wondered what had damaged Ruby's soul?

Misssissippi, she thought. She would go to Mississippi and bury her brother. She would talk to her sister Faye. She would find the missing piece of Ruby. There once had to be a girl of smiles, of joy, of love.

Neecey's tears flowed as the el rumbled from the South Side, from Ruby, and all the scars imprinted on her body, her memory, and her heart. At Thirty-fifth Street she looked toward Stateway Gardens, the housing project that had robbed her of her youth, her virginity, and all her girlhood illusions. She wrapped her arms around herself and closed her eyes. Neecey saw herself as a frightened, tortured little child.

"It's okay," she whispered to the child. "We're free. It's okay. You don't have to hurt anymore."

Neecey's Lullaby is the story of a young girl who grows into adulthood under the harshest of conditions, managing not only to survive but to become a surrogate mother to her younger siblings. The questions that follow are meant to spark conversation about Neecey's journey and the supporting cast of characters.

1. Jesse disappears from the novel by chapter 4 and does not reappear until chapter 16. What's the motivation for focusing on him in the first three chapters?

2. *Neecey's Lullaby* is set in the mid-1950s through early 1970s. Think about why the author might have chosen this time period instead of a more contemporary setting.

3. Della is aware of the beatings administered by Ruby. Why doesn't she interfere?

4. Miss Cole is concerned about Ruby's treatment of Neecey. Why doesn't she contact the authorities? What resources do today's teachers have to help abused children? What resources do family, neighbors, and children have?

What legal steps would be taken against a mother like Ruby today?

5. Throughout the novel, Ruby is in one bad relationship after another. How does this impact her relationship with the children? Which relationship or relationships are the children most comfortable with? Which relationship had the worse impact on the children? Why?

6. Knowing that Ruby chose the name Darcy Bane to reflect a poisonous relationship, why do you think she chose the names Serenda Joy and Jordan?

7. Although Ruby is abusive, Neecey often stands up to her. When and why?

8. After his accident, why does Manny think Ruby is the wrong person to care for him? Why is he upset that Neecey is moving?

9. In the final confrontation with Ruby, Jordan claims that Neecey has always been their mother. Why?

10. How would the novel change if it was told from Ruby's point of view? Odessa's point of view? Jack's point of view?

about the author

Cris Burks received her M.F.A. in creative writing from Columbia College in Chicago. She is the author of the novel *SilkyDreamGirl,* and her short stories and poems have appeared in many literary publications, including *Shooting Star Review* and *Short Fiction by Women* and the anthologies *Gumbo: A Celebration of Black Writers* and *The Thing About Love Is* . . . She lives in Sacramento, California.